A DUBIOUS ALLIANCE

First edition. October 31, 2024.

Copyright © 2024 Dumo Xaba.

ISBN: 979-8227216168

Written by Dumo Xaba.

DUMO XABA is a creative artist with a passion for storytelling both written and visual. Having found love for the arts at a young age, he is now an author, poet, photographer and filmmaker.

DUMO IS A FULL-TIME creative, dedicated to telling stories through novels, poetry, photography, and videography.

Find out more about Dumo Xaba and his literature:
Visit his website www.dumoxaba.co.za[1]

Written by hands made for the glory of God

A DUBIOUS
ALLIANCE

---

2. http://www.dumoxaba.co.za

PROLOGUE

KwaZulu Union Bay City, November 3rd, 2006

AN ORDINARY DAY FOR some, a life-changing Friday for many others. Before the recently opened city hall gathered a large crowd of expectant hopefuls. At a podium proudly stood the newly appointed mayor, on her left was newly appointed police captain, Mawande Dambuza, and on the right of the mayor was business tycoon, Zenzele Msani, who represented the five investors who financed the building of KwaZulu Union Bay City – who were later dubbed the Founding Five.

KwaZulu Union Bay City was certainly a city few could compare to. Located in the northeast region of KwaZulu-Natal, South Africa, it rested just a few minutes away from St. Lucia. The city, however, did not conform to most of the laws and practices of its location country, thanks to Msani who worked with a large team of lawyers to ensure the city's independence from the rest of the country. Some of the more notable differences are the heavier hand of the law, and the unwavering commitment of its enforcers, from the time of arrest, right to the jury's verdict, or the judge's, depending on the circumstance. This was one reason for the crime rate being extraordinarily low, another was the unspoken fact that crime was capitalised. One man had successfully become the unchallenged kingpin of crime, ensuring all criminal entities in the city fell under his rule, played by his rules, and none slipped through his fingers.

Adopting the moniker Using History to Creatively Innovate into the Future, the goal was for Union Bay to be the first of its kind in the country then be the foundation for other cities like it across the nation. Over the years, the government was only able to duplicate its success once, though on a smaller scale. That came in the form of the small town of Ster Nag Stad in the Northern Cape.

KwaZulu Union Bay was filled with artistically structured buildings such as the Shaka Museum of Zulu History, and the Union Sports Stadium, with skyscrapers from east to west. Two bullet trains, modelled from the Gautrain and improved upon, travelled from north to south, beneath the ground and in the air. Every house installed with customizable smart home appliances.

It has taken on many nicknames over the years such as Union Bay, the city of innovation, and the homeland of creativity, however the most popular according to an article on an annual survey was KUB City. The same article stated that the city is in the Top 10 destinations to visit in South Africa, noting its beaches as the second best in the country, bested only by the white sands of Cape Town.

The mayor looked over the great multitude with a pinch of pride in what was accomplished by the city. She tapped on the mic before speaking. "Ladies and gentlemen, boys and girls, people of all ages. We are here today thanks to the minds, and of course, the money of five individuals who envisioned the renewal of a city-wide deserted environment. A next-generation city from a place which was considered a wasteland..." she quickly stole a glance at Zenzele.

The business tycoon gave her a little nod.

"Without further ado, it brings me great pleasure to officially welcome you all to the first of the next generation of South African cities. Welcome to KwaZulu Union Bay City."

The crowd broke into applause as the mayor was handed a large pair of gold scissors, with which she cut the red ribbon at the door of the city hall, officially opening KwaZulu Union Bay City to the world.

CHAPTER 1

KwaZulu Union Bay City, October 31st, 2023

THE MAN BEGGED FOR mercy as he tried to pull himself upright in the dark alley. He had no way of escaping, but even if he did, there was no place to hide where he could not be found. He was surrounded by a group of three men and a woman, all dressed in grey waistcoats, trousers and overcoats. "Presentation demands respect, respect gives power," the boss would always say. He only had three rules he and those who worked for him were forced to follow. Respect your elders, always have a backup plan, and dress like you own the world.

"Please, stop. I will pay whatever he wants. I just need a little more time to get the money."

"This is not about money," one of the men responded. His attire was finished with a silver pocket watch which he had in hand to remain mindful of time. "This is about respect," his voice echoed, demonstrating his dominance.

"And you, don't seem to understand how that works," another added.

"You had a chance to pay back the money and you didn't. You made your bed, it's time to lay in it."

After checking his watch again, the leader stepped back. "Let's wrap it up," he instructed. The other two men closed in, but the leader stopped them. "Let the noob do it."

The men stepped aside.

The woman, who hadn't spoken or moved as yet looked to her instructor, turned to her other associates, then fixed her attention back on the man who was on his knees, helpless. She took a step forward, raised her hand and took a swing. From that very first punch, she felt her stomach turn. She accepted the situation and reminded herself that when the boss wants something done, it has to be done, no questions asked, no answers given. Again, she raised her hand as she got on a knee and took another swing. Right, then left, then right, and another left. She felt the urge to keep going boiling inside of her and she knew what it meant. She composed herself as she got to her feet. Gritting her teeth, she tossed the man to the feet of her associates.

The leader pulled out a gun, checked that it was loaded then aimed at the man at his feet.

"Wait." The woman could feel her heart jump to her throat as her leader focused his attention on her.

"I'm sorry, are you giving the orders now?"

"No. And I do not question you. But the king said to teach him some respect, not kill him."

"Okay then, please explain to me how exactly those two things are any different."

"Well, killing him won't change anything, besides leaving a trail of debt and bodies. But leaving him in this state sends a message. No one can hide from the king. And once he's back in full health, he will pay back everything he owes. With interest of course." She turned to the bleeding man. "Right?"

With his face half swollen, he nodded as best he could.

Mulling the words, he pulled his gun away. "Consider this a message to those who think they don't need to pay their dues. Long live the king." Using his gun he knocked the man to the ground, then lowered it.

The anxious woman could feel an internal sigh of relief.

"The boss would be impressed by your skills."

"Would be?"

"Yes," he turned to the woman. "Unfortunately, he won't be, because I'm not," he growled. "It's my job to ensure every employee is trustworthy. And you are not really giving me a trustworthy feeling. You negotiate like a cop. And you know what they say," he took a step forward. "If it walks like a duck, and quacks like a duck, it's a duck," he concluded, lifting his gun to Mandisa. Using his free hand, he pulled out his phone from his pocket.

"You're making a mistake."

"We're about to find out." After dialling, he held it to his ear. The phone rang.

A scream of agony reverberated on the walls of the alley and faded into the night. The handgun clattered on the ground. It was a shot to the wrist.

"Sniper," one of the gangmen shouted as he tried to make out where the shot came from while ducking to the ground.

The woman pulled out her gun, and took a few shots in the direction of where the sniper could be then she pulled the man who just held her at gunpoint by the arm, dragging him behind a large disposal bin. Quickly, she peeked from her hiding place and ducked back. A bullet hit the ground next to her.

"How convenient."

"Are you serious?" Ignoring his glare, she grabbed an old cloth from the side of the bin and wrapped it around the man's wrist.

"Ah!"

"Apply pressure and hope we make it out of here."

"We aren't. And I'm not going to jail."

"So what, you want to Kamikaze this?"

"It's better than nothing."

"It's really not."

"Gun."

Without thinking twice, one of the other men threw his gun to him and he caught it with his only good hand.

"Don't try to play cowboy."

The leader nodded to his crew, strained to get up and jumped out from his hiding place. Before he could pull the trigger, bullets ripped through his body till he hit the ground. All they could do was watch.

There were no sirens, no sound of engines, just the thundering of dozens of footsteps closing in on the alley. In moments, lights flooded the alley, flushing out the darkness enveloping the assailants.

"Hands up!" a voice called out. Behind the brightness of the lights, police officers zoned in on the perpetrators.

The other man, still having a gun in hand started panting heavily. He looked up.

"Don't do it."

The man got up and immediately received two bullets in the chest.

"You are a cop."

Cover blown, Detective Mandisa Xaba looked at the only survivor of the three men she started the night with and sighed. She looked up and shook her head. With a sigh, she got to her feet. "We're coming out, don't shoot."

An officer rushed to check on the injured victim. After a quick exam he looked up, "get the medic to check on him, and stay with him for the night," he instructed. Two officers helped the man up, one of them referring to the instructor as "detective".

Mandisa walked over to where the phone landed when the sniper shot for the first time.

"What were you thinking—"

Mandisa placed her finger on her mouth and pointed to the phone on the ground. She spun her finger around horizontally.

The detective froze for a moment. "Still on?" he mouthed.

Mandisa nodded.

"You shouldn't have taken money from the kingpin," he put on his best acting voice. "Get him out of here."

Mandisa slowly picked up the phone.

"That thing still on?" He waited for a second. "Turn it off."

Only then did Mandisa release a breath she didn't realize she was holding. "What are you doing here?"

"You mean besides saving your behind?"

"I had it under control."

"It looked like the only thing you had was a death wish."

Mandisa turned her attention to the injured man as he was pulled away on a stretcher. She wasn't comfortable with the situation she was in, but she understood that it was the job. Part of being undercover was not blowing your identity, and she knew that if she wanted to get the big boss at the top of the food chain, she had to swallow every bite of humanity she had and play her role. She already knew that tonight was a waste, the kingpin wouldn't trust her again. "We're going to talk about this tomorrow."

CHAPTER 2

KwaZulu Union Bay City, November 1st, 2023

KICKING AND SCREAMING a man was dragged into the Union Bay City Police Station. The floor bustled with activity as the officers attended members of the public, while others busied themselves with piles of paperwork, casually chatting as they sifted through their workload.

Deep into the station, in an office, the door of which had a plank reading, Detective Xaba, the young woman sat behind her table, her left hand holding her phone to her ear while her right hand streaked a pen across her notepad. "Okay, okay, thank you so much. And if you remember anything else, relevant or not, you have my number. Thanks, enjoy the rest of your day." She hung up as she finished short-handing some notes. Satisfied with the information gathered, the detective turned her attention to her computer.

The door burst open to reveal a fuming older man in a blue shirt and khaki pants, flanked by Detective Thabiso Simelane, almost startling the detective out of her chair. "Xaba!" the man yelled.

Trying to suppress an angry sigh Mandisa responded, "Kapteni."

He slammed the door shut and walked over to the detective's table. "What happened yesterday?" he asked resting his fists on the table and leaning forward.

I could ask you the same thing, the detective thought of responding. But she also knew better than to add fuel to the flame at the station, and Sithole, the captain, was already fuming. "My cover, which I have worked months to build, was blown because of the ambush."

"Oh no, we are not going to ignore what happened before that. You assaulted a civilian. Since when do you get to lay a hand on an innocent man?"

"A person of interest," the detective corrected.

"Wrong. The answer is never," the captain slammed his fist into the table.

"I was on the job," she rose from her seat to look her superior in the eye. Their relationship had been very rocky, for the most part, usually because she could spontaneously use some rather unorthodox methods to "get the job done."

Sithole never liked that approach, he was a hard man of the law, known to do everything by the book and no other way. He considered himself one very old dog you couldn't teach new tricks.

"And if I didn't do it, they would've suspected me."

"They suspected you regardless," Thabiso added.

"Don't," Mandisa pointed at her colleague. There's a lot she thought about saying to Thabiso at that moment. Of all the people she couldn't get along with at the station, he was at the top of the list. There was always tension between the two of them, being the best detectives at the station. To make matters worse for Mandisa, all the men usually took Thabiso's side on any and every disagreement they had over the years. "You have no place to speak here."

"I beg to differ," Thabiso replied.

"Well, it's a good thing your option does not matter in this case."

"Enough! Both of you are acting worse than dramatic high school kids," Sithole sighed. "Mandisa, there's a line. There is a line that we don't ever cross, and that line exists for good reason. You crossed that line."

"I know, but if I didn't, we wouldn't have that man in holding right now. And we wouldn't have the direct contact to the kingpin."

"The man in holding, that's just lovely, isn't it? Well done on that accomplishment, but you can tell that to the man fighting for his life at Union Bay General."

"Fighting for—" her frustration built up. She closed her eyes stealing a moment of silence. She was aware that the captain ignored the second part of what she said but she knew not to dwell on that. "It was merely a few punches. They hardly qualify to even be—"

"What?" the captain interrupted. "To even be what, Mandisa? Murder?"

Mandisa bowed her head with a sigh as she realized the trap she walked into.

"Well. Because you clearly didn't do a good enough 'job', the man you beat up was attacked in his home at eleven last night and beat to a pulp."

"What?"

"The officers that I had assigned to watch over him were found tied to the washing line in the backyard with the message, 'You think you can make a difference, but you can't. You want to catch me, but you work for me without even realizing it.'" The captain concluded, dropping the note he was reading from on the table.

Mandisa looked at the note, then turned to her colleague. "You shouldn't have interfered."

"You can't possibly be serious," Thabiso replied. "Are you trying to say that this is my fault? I'm the last person you can blame for this."

"If it wasn't for you—"

"If I didn't green light Thabiso, you and your little posse would've killed the man. And you would've been an accomplice to murder."

"They wouldn't have killed him."

"And how would you know that?"

"Because they needed him. I wasn't sure for what yet, but it's going to be harder to find out now."

"With any luck, we'll never have to find out." After a moment of thought, Sithole sighed. "In fact, it won't be harder for you to find out, it will be impossible. As of this moment, you're off the cartel case."

"What? Sithole!"

"Kapteni," Sithole corrected.

"It's my case!"

"Then you should've thought about that before you gambled with another man's life!"

Mandisa turned away, trying to swallow her anger.

"Thabiso, you will be taking over the case... with immediate effect."

When Mandisa's gaze returned, Thabiso felt a bit of intimidation kick in. His eyes darted away.

"Mandisa please give everything you have regarding the case, including," Sithole emphasized, "whatever information you were able to discover about the Kingpin to Thabiso before the end of the day." Without waiting for a response, he stormed out, leaving the door open.

Without lifting his head, Thabiso could still feel Mandisa's gaze on him. "I'd appreciate it if those files were on my desk as soon as possible."

"I thought you were a detective."

"I am."

"Then detect your way out of my office, and do your job."

Thabiso couldn't look Mandisa in the eyes again because if looks could kill, he'd be dead he thought. After walking out, he closed the door behind himself.

And a split second later, every person in the station turned to the detective's office at the sound of glass shattering on wood. This was followed by an echoing silence.

Detective Mandisa Xaba was not a difficult person, she just hated being undermined and disrespected. It did not help that most of her colleagues were full of themselves and very proud of their achievements, particularly Thabiso. She could deal with being a woman in a man's world, the favouritism, nepotism and lowkey sexism she experienced as one-third of the women who worked at the station. But there was just one thing she dreaded most about her life; she was too white for black people and too black for white people. A rather backward way of thinking for such an advanced city. Regardless of her father being Zulu and mother being Xhosa, her manner of speech made her sound "white" according to the guy from the Libalele Grillers drive-thru two years ago. That comment infuriated her so much that she couldn't stop herself from responding, "Guess you can blame my parents for trying to give me the best life they could afford." From the day she was born, there were this or that perceptions about her due to her appearance. Zulu or Xhosa? Black or coloured? She looked rather young for her age which suited her just fine, but what she didn't appreciate was the unwanted attention her hourglass-like figure would draw as she entered a room.

CHAPTER 3

AFTER DUMPING A FEW case files on Simelane's desk, Mandisa went to Union Bay City General Hospital. Being the hospital that Sithole was referring to by "Union Bay General", she knew it was the one she would find the man in – considering the captain was telling the truth. With the mere flash of her badge, she was attended to by a nurse who showed her to the room she was looking for. To her horror, Sithole made no exaggeration about the condition of the man; Bayanda Zondi according his chart. He was beaten and bruised on the side of his face not covered by the bandage wrapped around the other half of his head. The only reason he was still alive was because of the machine he was plugged into. Bullets of sweat were beginning to flow down the detective's face as she choked back some tears. She looked back at the chart, it confirmed everything Sithole had told her.

"Hello," called out a voice. "Are you family?"

Mandisa turned to the source of the question, only then did she realize her hand was shaking. "No," she choked. With a breath, she calmed herself.

"Well, I'm glad I caught a face he might recognize; he has to drink some medication in a few minutes, so I brought his food." The nurse placed the tray on the table in front of the bed. "Maybe you could help, I'm sure he'd appreciate it more than he does for any of us nurses to do it for him," she stood on the side of the bed, looking over the man. "After all, we are just strangers to him. Mr Zondi," the nurse called out. "There's someone here to see you."

Bayanda stirred and winced. Flinching as he blinked with his one eye.

"I forgot to ask," the nurse turned, only then realizing the woman had disappeared.

WITH DETERMINATION in her step, the detective stormed down the hallway of the hospital. She couldn't help the flashes of last night she kept remembering. The screams of the man as her fists met his face. The heat of her blood pumping through her veins. She was only just realizing that she was losing control. However, her thoughts were disturbed by the noise from a small group huddled in the corner watching the television hanging on the wall. Her feet pulled to a stop as she turned her attention to the screen as the Union Bay Newsroom Live Emergency Broadcast alert looped on it. The alert faded to black as the sound of breathing came through. The screen remained this way for a few moments... then a figure stepped into the frame. Dressed in a well-designed slim cut full black three-piece suit and hat with a balaclava covering the person's face.

Slowly, a very husky voice began, "KwaZulu... Union... Bay... City."
The man exhaled. "We are a few days away from the 17th Anniversary of the city. And to celebrate this year, I have planned a series of challenges to be solved. If you would be so kind as to indulge me for a few moments, I won't take up too much of your time." A deafening pause. "Five they were, four now, soon three. A city's success built on lies and fees. What happens when the truth comes out?" The figure took slow sickening steps towards the camera, his mask-covered face filling the frame before he continued. "For the next two days, there will be four challenges, at the end of one, another will be issued, his head moved around the screen as he continued. "Everyone is welcome to participate, as they say, the more, the merrier. This is your first challenge to solve." He turned from the camera, then when he turned back, the words he spoke, layered above his face. "I cheat, rob and kill, infamous

and crowned, what am I?" the words faded off the screen. "Solve the riddle and save a life, although, I'm not sure you'll want to. You have six hours." And with that, the screen faded to black.

This was followed by divisions of light panic and chatter. A Union Bay Newsroom Live presenter in the newsroom studio cut onto the screen, grabbing the attention of some of the doctors and nurses. The city had experienced its fair share of crime wars, psychopaths, sadists and terrorist threats.

However, this felt different for the detective. Disregarding her surroundings, Mandisa focused on the words that were spoken, trying to memorize as much as she could remember. She figured if she couldn't keep pursuing the cartel case, she could give this riddle a try and see where it would lead her. As the only female detective in that part of the city and one of the best undercover, she knew she had nothing to prove – to others at least.

CHAPTER 4

AS SOON AS MANDISA got back to her car, her phone pinged in her pocket. Pulling it out, she double-tapped on the message from **James (KUPS)**.

Look alive boys, we have a new crazy on the loose, and you know what we do to crazies. Let's find this joker and put him in the looney bin before he strikes.

A message from Thabiso, sent on the group.

Mandisa knew the group James was referring to. They called it the **KUB City Strike Team**. It was a group of seven officers from the station that Thabiso – who created the group – considered to be the best. James was one of the seven, not that he wanted to be. It was Mandisa who had convinced him not to leave it as it could have its benefits; advancing his career, getting him cases, being in the inner circle at the station Mandisa had listed for him. He argued that to be "favouritism." Mandisa never responded to that; he was the first white male she ever met to complain about favouritism.

Her phone pinged again.

It's about the guy who just made an announcement on TV, not sure if you saw it.

Another ping.

Thabiso and Jabu have been assigned the case.

Mandisa silenced her phone after sending James a "Thank you" message, then stole a moment to herself. This was not the first time James forwarded Mandisa a message from the KUB City Strike Team group. It had become frequent for him to do so, almost religious. This allowed Mandisa to help him help the team solve cases while also giving her access to information she wouldn't have otherwise. Additionally, Mandisa would help James with his cases, or ensure that he's assigned the right cases. An agreement that had begun when James first got to the station. He was new and the captain hadn't thought he could trust him as yet, so he partnered him with Mandisa. She tried to refuse because she had never started working with a partner and that suited her well. Regardless, Sithole insisted. So, she taught him what she knew, he respected her, and they worked well together... until Mandisa started pursuing the cartel case. James pleaded with the captain to take him off the case until he agreed.

Mandisa shook off the memory as she drove home. She knew it wasn't wise to continue pursuing the cartel case after Sithole handed it over to Thabiso, but they both should know her better by now, she thought.

Later that night, after a small supper, Mandisa returned to the living room where she caught a few moments of the news. She wasn't surprised that the media already gave the riddle man a nickname; *The Premeditator*, and that the police had opened an investigation into it, also asking for the public's help in any way – perhaps if someone recognized the voice or the location. What they hadn't asked for was anyone who recognized the suit. Thabiso and Jabu were still as good as average she thought. The suit looked specially tailored. Which meant finding the tailor would be a great lead. Aware of what may come of her actions, she disregarded the consequences because she knew that if she let Thabiso and Jabu – along with the team of their choosing – take care of it, possibly nothing would happen. Her mind went back to Sithole's words, "Then you should've thought about that before you gambled with another man's life!" She dismissed the thought and realized how frustrated she was getting, so she did the only thing she knew would get rid of the flashbacks she was getting; she interrogated the riddle.

"I cheat, rob and kill, infamous and crowned, what am I?"

Her initial guess was criminal. But that wouldn't stick with the second part of the riddle; infamous and crowned. So, she started thinking broader, could be a banker? Unlikely to be a killer. Cop? Possibly, – and she spent a while weighing which of her colleagues it could be (particularly Aryan Chetty, she just didn't think she could trust someone who was able to easily get into the mind of a killer and dissect how someone was killed) – but something wasn't adding up. If this so-called Premeditator was already living up to that name, it couldn't be some random person. Televising themselves was a calculated move, they – whoever he or she is – wanted to be seen and heard, and they wanted everyone's attention for whatever sick game they're playing at.

That's when Mandisa realized it. Though she knew her guess couldn't be absolute and she could be very wrong, she was getting a feeling that she wasn't far from the bullseye. "'Five they were, four now, soon three.' It could only be one group of people; the Founding Five. It had to be. But could one of them be a killer? Is it possible that all of them could be killers, or even just dangerous? Criminals? Is that why they never revealed their identities to the public? Mandisa now had more questions than answers and the only person who could answer them died well over a year ago. That being wealthy business tycoon, the late Zenzele Msani.

Msani was the face of the five and as to whom the rest of the Founding Five were was mostly a mystery no one ever looked into. They were the people who built the city, financially speaking, no one questioned that. The only person whose identity was public knowledge was the Five's public face; Msani. His death dropped the five to four, and in doing so, it made investigating who the remaining four are very difficult. But one thing was certain, they are rich, powerful and clearly famous. Or in this case infamous. Every cop in the city knew that there was only one crowned king of crime in Union Bay, 'the Kingpin'. Mandisa was already on her feet, rushing to the garage, where she kept her many files of information collected over her past seven years on the force, most of which she was not supposed to have. She ruffled through the boxes she thought she'd find an answer in, making a mess of the place before finding the piece of paper with the single detail she was looking for.

93 JR Hills Avenue.

It was the only perk she thought she had of working at the station; no one really paid all that much attention to her thus allowing her to retrieve whatever information she needed without eyes and ears watching and listening. Without thinking, she was already in her car, racing to the location.

CHAPTER 5

THE DETECTIVE ARRIVED at the location as quickly as her car could take her (breaking the speed limit a few times in the parts of the highway she knew there were no speed cameras). Having parked a short walk away from the secluded mansion, Mandisa tracked just within the edge of the surrounding forest to get to the unfenced and unguarded property. As she stepped onto the property, her stomach turned as she remembered all the bad things she'd heard that the owner had done over the years. The robberies he had planned, the police he'd turned, the drugs he flooded the streets with, and worst of all, his slow, agonizing methods of torture and killing.

Finding the front door ever so slightly open, Mandisa tried to be as stealthy as possible – though the golden tips of her hair were not helping her in this endeavour – she slowly pulled out her Baretta m9 to have it ready for anything as she tiptoed through the house. The old double story was quiet – as quiet as a house in the woods could be at least. Then... the creaking of wood. She stopped and looked at her feet, squinting in the dark to ensure she didn't step on any other bad flooring. She calmed herself before continuing. The living room was empty, and so was the rest of the house she thought in hope. She raised her gun as she approached the only lit room on the floor, down the hall to the right. The kitchen. She leaned against the wall, peaking her head around the corner. The door was open, letting in short bursts of chilling air. The kitchen was well decorated, black and white, with tiles from roof to floor. Granite countertops and pure white wooden cupboards. She turned the corner, gun raised and moved with quick heel-to-toe steps through the modern kitchen, circled the island counter then stopped at the door to take a knee. Her eyes darted around the darkness enveloping the thick forest. She could see no movement, nor hear a sound but the wind crashing through the trees. Getting to both feet, she swept the door closed. Returning to the counters, she looked at the vast array of products before a red water-diluted liquid in the slick white sink caught her eye. Upon closer inspection, she knew it was blood, but not enough to trace it back to the source. But where there was blood, someone was bleeding. The detective raised her firearm once more and returned to the hallway. This time around, she noticed an adjure door that was letting in the smallest light. With a deep breath, she used her body to push the door open.

A slight odour washed over her nose, and she instantly recognized the smell. As she froze in place, time almost seemed to stop. As if something took over her body, she moved slowly and steadily into the office, unmistakably recognizing the man lying in a pool of his blood – the city's crowned king of crime, the man she was working to catch for the past nine months, the one whose case she was taken off of hours ago. His eyes were still wide open as if in a state of shock. Usually, the detective would be glad to be right, but she was coming to regret this dreaded night as it was unfolding before her.

He did it, she thought. Whoever this "Premeditator" person is, they must have a serious grudge against the Founding Five to have left a statement like this. It was beyond horrifying. And the thought that the media would be all over this in no more than 48 hours concerned the detective. As she dialled the station on her phone she realized that her hands were trembling and her voice shaking as she spoke. "This is Detective Mandisa Xaba... I need... I need a team at uhm... 9... 93 JR Hills... Avenue."

She took a minute to compose herself. After which she moved like a woman on a mission. To find something. She didn't know what, but she knew there had to be something missing, something broken, something out of place, something that indicated someone else was there. She needed to find something before the on-duty officers arrived. Regardless of her profession and rank, she knew exactly what the situation looked like for her, so she needed said proof to prove her innocence. She knew that right at that moment, it looked like she was angry about being taken off the cartel case, so she went and killed the man at the top of the cartel.

She rushed to the kitchen and used her shirt to pull open all the drawers to avoid leaving her fingerprints. The first two drawers had cutlery and cooking instruments. She found what she was searching for in the third drawer; a packet of small 20x30cm plastics. She pulled two out and used them as gloves for her hands. After closing the drawers, she hurried back to the home office to look through the files on the table, the table drawers, and the bookshelf. The last drawer was locked, she looked at the body on the floor. She thought that was the only place she would find the key to open the drawer, but she didn't want to get any closer to the corpse than she already was. Not to mention, moving the body would be considered as altering the crime scene. She sighed. She couldn't find anything useful.

The detective thought about heading upstairs. She slipped her shoes off to avoid making noise and rushed up the stairs, peaking at each of the rooms as she walked by the open doors until she got to what she assumed to be the master bedroom. As she stepped into the room, she noted how neat it was. She knew she had to keep it that way, so she pulled out her phone and took a few pictures of the room. Once she was satisfied with them, she slipped her phone back into her pocket and started looking around at possible hiding places. She checked the wardrobe, then the bed, and the bedside compartments. When she took a step back, she noticed a faint glinting on the wall opposite the large bedroom window. She turned the flash of her phone on and approached the wall. The glinting was caused by a small circular piece of medal hidden in the wall. She pulled on the medal, and it opened the wall, revealing a walk-in closet. With a scoff, she entered. Luxury watches, red bottom shoes and designer suits filled the room. She took a moment to assess the suits, then thought back to the suit the Premeditator was wearing. Too similar to not be the same tailor she thought, so she counted the hangers that didn't have any suits. Two. The kingpin is wearing one suit, which means another is missing. The detective considered that it could be possible that the kingpin was killed before the Premeditator's video. But only the autopsy would tell.

The drawers had a glass on top of them to allow you to see what's inside. All the drawers were the same size, except one. One was deeper than the rest, but its contents were at the same level as all the others. Mandisa realized it had a secret compartment. She ran her pinkie finger along the sides and corners of the black velvet perfectly fitted on the bottom of the drawer. On the right corner closest to her, her finger fell into a small gap. With much care, she pulled the velvet-covered piece of wood out. It was the first messy place in the house. File folders, loose documents, and bank statements filled the hidden compartment. She pulled a few out and started reading through them. She didn't understand much from the bank statements, but she noticed that most of them belonged to the accounts of other people. Still immersed in studying the documents, Mandisa was disturbed by the sound of approaching sirens. She replaced the things she had moved around, stepped out of the closet and closed it. Before she rushed downstairs she pulled out her phone to check how the room looked in comparison to the images she took when she stepped in. Not seeing anything out of place, she ran down the stairs, slipped her shoes back on, and pasted on a horrified face as she stepped outside to wait on the steps outside the front door.

DUMO XABA

AS THE POLICE CRUISERS screeched into the driveway, a car the colour of teeth in a toothpaste advert pulled up behind them, and from it emerged a rather short chestnut-toned man. Rushing towards the house as quickly as his legs could get him, he hit the shutter of his pocket-sized camera as fast as it would allow him as he manoeuvred around the cruisers before their drivers had a chance to step out. He was quick. However, before he could reach his destination, he was halted by the captain, a sour expression playing on his face.

"Get him out of here," shrieked the new lead detective of the cartel case, Thabiso Simelane. An order to which two officers complied, struggling to lead the fighting man back to his car.

Mandisa could feel the man's camera zoom in to frame her face as she tried to cover it. Meeting her captain at the bottom of the stairs, she began, "Sir, we have..."

"Did I not tell you to stay away from the cartel case? No, don't answer that. I don't understand how much clearer I have to be with you. What is it you have against this man?"

"I wasn't pursuing the cartel case."

"Then what are you doing here?"

"Following another lead."

"That coincidently led you to the man I wanted you to stay away from."

The detective looked away, naturally feeling that Sithole didn't believe her.

He brushed his hand over his brow as he glanced at the approaching officers. "I think you should go home, get some rest and we'll talk tomorrow, okay?"

"Yeah, the big boys are here now," remarked Thabiso as he walked into the house.

Mandisa listened to his footsteps fade into the darkness before she proceeded. "With all due respect, sir... I solved the riddle; I found the body."

"Riddle, what riddle?"

"The Premeditator."

Sithole looked at the detective, tilting his head to the side as he considered her words. With a deep sigh, he massaged his forehead. "Look," he shook his head and sighed again. "I assigned that case to Thabiso and Jabu."

"I'm well aware sir, but I doubt they were getting anywhere with their investigation."

"Mandisa—"

"Tell me I'm wrong."

Sithole's eyes darted away from Mandisa before returning to her gaze.

"Put me on the case."

Sithole scoffed, taken by surprise for a moment. "I can't do that," he shook his head.

"Why not?"

"Look around. The song you're singing and the song everyone else will be singing are not the same thing. I..." the captain stopped himself as another group of officers rushed past them. "I can't just... give you the case, not even if I wanted to, I can't. It's impossible."

Thabiso stepped out of the house, flanked by Jabu. "Sorry to disturb your conversation, but can we ask you a few questions Mandisa?"

Mandisa and Sithole shared a look before turning to their colleagues.

"Yeah, sure."

"What time did you get here?"

"I don't know, half an hour ago, almost an hour ago maybe, I don't know," she shrugged.

"And what time did you get home?"

"Around twelve, give or take ten minutes."

"So, you stopped somewhere on the way?"

"Yes, Union Bay General."

"Can anyone attest to that?"

"I don't know, there was a nurse who helped me, I don't know if she'll remember me."

Thabiso and Jabu looked at each other, a question clearly playing on their minds, but they didn't ask.

"And you found the body in the state it's in," said Jabu.

"Obviously."

"Perhaps not as obvious as you think."

"What are you tryna say?"

"Where were you today around six?" Thabiso asked.

"How is that relevant?" She read the expression on Thabiso's face. "You think *I'm* behind this."

"It doesn't matter what I think. What matters is the truth, and right now, it's looking a lot like you left the station angry earlier today after being taken off the case. Sorry, after the case was given to me."

"And now you're here," Jabu completed. "In the home of the very man you were told to stop investigating."

"You can't be serious."

"Yeah, I think let's hold off on any accusations until we have our facts straight," Sithole stepped in.

"We're not accusing anyone," Thabiso responded. "We're just looking at the situation."

"Trying to get all the facts."

"I don't think Mandisa is in any shape to be answering any questions right now."

"Sir, you know how it is."

"Yeah, well, I'm saying let's not make it how it is tonight, okay? We'll see her at the station tomorrow and all the cards will be put on the table."

"We just wanted to get her perspective of what happened here," Jabu explained. "She was first on scene; from her theory, we could just fill in the blanks."

"Does she look like she wants to talk right now?"

"No sir."

"No. So could we save the questions for tomorrow."

"So, what do we do now?"

"What do you mean? We do our jobs and investigate what we have," Sithole indicated to the house. He turned to Mandisa. "Go home, get some rest."

"Sir—"

"She's not leaving the country; she's just going home, okay, detective?"

Thabiso nodded. "Yes, captain."

"Okay, I'll see you inside." Sithole led Mandisa down the short steps to walk her to her car. Once they were out of earshot, he spoke, "Look. I can't give you the case."

Mandisa stopped to look at the captain.

"However, if a concerned civilian decides to investigate this so-called Premeditator, I have no jurisdiction to stop them."

"Are you saying—"

"I'm not saying anything," he smiled.

Following the Captain's orders, Mandisa stepped into her car and drove home in complete quiescence.

It was only once she had put her head to her pillow, staring at the ceiling that her mind started buzzing with voices and images. The words of the Premeditator, the gruesomely murdered body, the countless documents she found in the hidden closet, and the captain's final words to her before she drove home. This was shaping out to be a huge case, and KwaZulu Union Bay City's greatest PR nightmare.

She sat up with a sigh. She pulled open her bedside drawer and dug through its neatly organised contents till she found a diary she had yet to use. Along with the rest beneath it, it was waiting for the pages in her current diary to get used up. At the beginning of every year, she'd buy three. By the end of the year, only two would be used up and the other left for years to come. The detective found solace in journaling all her cases. Writing out the official report for a case was never something she looked forward to, but journaling about the cases had become somewhat of a joyful habit. However, that's not something she would've ever admitted to her therapist, given that she was the one who advised Mandisa to start journaling. She grabbed a pen, shut the drawer, and sat with her legs crossed in the centre of the bed. She twirled the pen in her hand considering her words.

Hey, I hope this finds you well.

Mandisa reconsidered the words, then tore out the page. She spent a while looking at the blank page before her, which awaited the words she could not find. The clock above the doorway of her room continued to echo its ticks as her mind scrambled for the right words. Finally, pen met paper again.

Hey, it's Mandisa. You may find it a surprise to hear from me, but this was bound to catch up to us at some point. We always see each other from a distance, from the shadows of reality. And I understand that we've never been able to see eye to eye in the past, but I believe it's time we did. I hope you share that sentiment.

You'll probably want to know why now. I need your help because I don't think I can solve this one without you. So please get back to me as soon as you can. If not to help me then do it for yourself. We're in trouble.

She signed at the bottom of the page and closed the diary. Hopeful and anxious for a response, she placed the diary on her bedside drawer, and the pen on top of it then rested her head on her pillow. The voices were finally silent as she shut her eyes.

CHAPTER 6

KwaZulu Union Bay City, November 2nd, 2023

THE WIND WAS RATHER crisp the following morning in Union Bay. Which didn't help the nervousness the detective was feeling following the events of the previous night. Even with hours of sleep, she still couldn't shake the brutality she had seen. It was like nothing she had ever seen before, not in person at least. The closest comparison was the blood-filled, brutal scenes of a horror movie. When she turned to her right, she noticed the diary wasn't completely closed. The pen was left in between some pages. Willing herself up, she grabbed the diary and flipped it open.

The writing was sloppier than hers, a bit less cursive and the pen was clearly pressed much heavier on the page than she would like. She discarded the thought so she could read.

You reached out to me then expect me to respond for my own sake. Thinking or believing that I need your help is where you're very much mistaken. I know who you are Mandisa. You're the reason my memories are filled with more blackouts than moments I experienced. Nevertheless, I will help you, but only under two conditions.

Do you accept?

The conditions were not listed. Mandisa groaned. It's a game of trust she thought. It was either trust someone who has proven to be unreliable or hope for the best. One choice was more practical than the other, but both were still a massive gamble. The only difference was the people they would affect. With a sigh, she took hold of the pen, but all she was able to write was...

I

Then her hand trembled. She dropped the pen. Once again, considering her options. She couldn't afford to take this decision lightly. There was too much to risk without enough information. She was finally facing her greatest fear, and it terrified her.

MANDISA KNEW THINGS would be rather awkward at the station today, but from the second she stepped in, all eyes were on her. For the second day in a row, she was the cause of the agonizing silence in the station. She tried to get to her office without drawing any further attention, however, a voice stopped her before she could make it to her destination. "Xaba," the captain called out again from down the hall. "A word."

Turning to see the captain standing outside an interrogation room, Mandisa knew what was about to follow, and realized there was no use delaying the inevitable. She looked around the station, every face looking away from her glance.

As she stepped into the room, she noticed a face she didn't recognize. A man seated on the other side of the table, dressed in a grey two-piece suit, his hat placed at the corner of the table to make room for the contents of the folder placed square in front of him. The door was slammed once Mandisa was fully inside.

"Detective," the man began with a rather low growl-like voice. "Please take a seat."

Mandisa made no objection. She was determined to say as little as she could, knowing very well what was happening.

"Can I call you Mandisa?"

"Do you believe in what you're gonna try to do?"

"And what's that?"

Mandisa assessed the man's attire. "You're not a cop. You're just a guy who they call when something needs to be done. You have no idea who I am or how I'm feeling yet you will sit there and pretend you understand me."

"Perhaps, or maybe I'm just trying to help."

"Me, or the person you're taking orders from?"

The man smiled. "Your captain mentioned that you're quite the witty one. And in my experience, wit comes with a great mind. What do you think I'm trying to do here?"

"Trying to pin the murder on me." She tilted her head to look at the two-way mirror as if she could see right through it. Though she couldn't see him, she could imagine the captain shifting in one spot.

"Miss Xaba..."

"Detective." She could tell that her questioner was not used to being challenged – he was used to being in control – but there was nothing usual about Mandisa.

"Detective. My name is Thembinkosi Malinga. I'm told that you found the body of Mkhonto yesterday?" He slowly opened his folder. "Is that correct?" He looked up still expecting a response, but it never came. "Ma—Detective. I can only help you if you let me."

I don't need your help, Mandisa thought, *nor did I ask for it*. But she still wasn't willing to give the man the satisfaction of responding to his questions.

"How about this... I will try to paint the scene, just shake your head if I'm wrong, okay?" he persisted. "Yesterday, you, like many others saw the arrival shall we call it, of the so-called 'Premeditator' he air quoted with his fingers. And with your detective instincts kicking in, you decided to solve his riddle. Can you tell me how you figured out the answer?" He watched the detective, hoping at the least her mouth would twitch indicating that she wanted to say something, but she remained still and silent. "You do realize how bad things are looking for you?"

For the first time since she stepped into the room, Mandisa saw something in the questioner's eyes that gave her something of gladness – she saw doubt. She knew he was losing control of the situation, trying and failing to find a way forward, he was cracking, and the nerves were starting to show.

"How many innocent people have you interrogated Mr Malinga?"

"I don't normally have to interrogate innocent people." Regardless of the change of subject, he was glad the detective was starting to speak.

"Then how do you decide who's guilty?"

"That's not my job."

"Not your job. What is your job?"

"To find the truth."

"Right. Did you know that there are about 34 indicators of a person who is lying?"

"Yes, I did."

"Did you know probably more than half of those are visible in nervous people?"

"That I didn't know."

"So you're saying you never know when someone is lying, or if they're genuinely nervous." She noticed him shift slightly in his seat. "Are you a family man Mr Malinga?"

"I have a wife and kids, yes."

"How many people that you interrogated; do you think have families, or had families?"

"I don't know."

"You don't know because there's too many to remember, or you don't know because you choose not to remember?"

"I don't know because I don't know!" he sighed. "But I have a job to do, and I would appreciate it if we could get back to it." He now removed a blank page from his folder, revealing images from last night's scene.

Mandisa's breathing became heavier, her head shaking. She looked away.

"Detective. I really do want to understand what happened. How you may or may not have solved the riddle leading you to the house of Mkhonto." He didn't remove his gaze from Mandisa as he shifted the images across the table. "According to the details I was given, you were the first person on the scene, and you called it in. But before you could do that, someone else reported suspicious activity in the neighbourhood minutes before you could contact the station."

"That's impossible, nobody..." As Mandisa started to regret responding, she knew it was too late to take her words back. There was no indication that someone else was there since she closed the kitchen door and the little blood residue that she found in the sink was probably washed out by the time her colleagues arrived on scene. This was the reason she never wanted to entertain the man's questions to begin with. But that's when the realization struck her. This so-called "Premeditator" was not just watching, listening, and waiting, but they were pulling the strings. It wasn't just the city's attention they wanted, it was Mandisa's attention, and now they had it, although that's something they might come to regret she thought.

"I understand that this is difficult for you, but—"

"Have you ever been to a crime scene before?"

Caught off guard, he stared at her for a moment before answering. "No, not particularly," he responded blinking more times than normal.

"Then you don't understand."

"Mandi—" he sighed. "Detective. Help me help you, please. What happened yesterday?"

"Will you believe me?" Shifting her gaze to the two-way mirror again, "Will they believe me?"

"Detective... You are the photographer here. You have the bigger picture. We're the audience, looking at pieces of the puzzle, trying to see what you see."

"You didn't answer my question."

"I have no reason not to believe you."

Mandisa was now willing to talk, but she still didn't trust the man seated squarely in front of her. She explained how she solved the riddle, taking short breaks between her sentences. Though she didn't mention how she knew the address of the Kingpin, she told him that when she got there and found the body, she called it in immediately then waited for her colleagues to arrive, which was at least half true. She didn't want to mention the snooping as she knew very well how that would not help her case.

After a few more questions, trying to understand all the information the detective gave him, Thembinkosi returned all the images to the folder, thanked Mandisa for her time and left the room as Sithole came in.

"Go home. Take the day off, clear your head, and do whatever you have to do, then come back ready to work tomorrow," the captain explained.

CHAPTER 7

AT UNION BAY CITY NEWS, the floor bustled with activity as the journalists tried to submit their articles, photographers their images, and the interns trafficked to and fro. Investigative journalist, Mpho Seme, manoeuvred through the crowd to the editor's office. As usual, dressed in a jean and a long-sleeved shirt. His brush cut was no longer as short and as fresh as he liked to keep it.

With a knock on the door, he let himself in. "Sir, you wanted to see me."

The editor looked up, his face turning a shade redder. "Close the door and sit down," the editor replied.

Mpho did as instructed. "Is something wrong?" He could see the concern on his supervisor's face.

"What do you think Mpho? Hmm? Tell me- tell me... what you think is wrong."

"Wish I could sir."

"Stop calling me sir."

"Sorry."

Sir and ma'am were as wired into Mpho as please and thank you. His mother made sure of that. It was a sign of respect she taught him. "If you respect others, they'll be trusting enough to respect you," she would always say. He remembered those words throughout his career.

"With all due respect," Mpho continued. "I don't understand how that could be such a big problem."

"It's not the problem."

"Then if you don't mind my asking si—" he exhaled. "If you don't mind my asking, what is the problem?"

"The article Mpho, the article!"

His eyebrows almost connected, his eyes narrowing. It was unusual for the editor to complain about his articles. If there was one person who barely needed supervision, it was Mpho Seme. His articles were always engaging and insightful. At times dangerous perhaps, but he felt they were necessary. Someone had to tell the difficult stories. The stories no one else dared come close to. At times, they were controversial, and he never would deny that. He understood what dangers he put himself in every time he published an article. He grew accustomed to hate mail and verbal and written threats. At one point in time, he was attacked in his home and held at gunpoint along with his daughter, Hayley, and her mother, Melissa Oosthuizen, who later moved out and left the city. She wanted to take Hayley with her, but she couldn't, the bond of dad and daughter was too strong. So, she came to an agreement with Mpho, if things got too heated, Hayley would move in with her. The break-in made Mpho rethink his profession. However, two days later, he was back in the office because he learned one thing from the attack; if someone was feeling threatened, he was clearly doing his job right. He was on the radar of every type of figure in town, political leaders, business CEOs, and even gang bosses. In most cases, he was the reason anyone thought twice before working with you in Union Bay. So as far as investigative journalists go, Mpho knew he was one of the best in the city, his colleagues knew it too.

"What about the article? It can't be the spelling, I triple-checked, and the structure is..."

"Stop."

For a moment the journalist remained silent. He didn't enjoy silence, he had an issue with not doing anything, and that's why he spoke so much. So much so that he mastered small talk. "Is it about my source, because I can assure you, he's a reliable cop, I can vouch for him any day of the week."

"Mpho!" a mere breath later, the editor was panting. Sliding his drawer open, he pulled out a container and swallowed its contents. He took a moment to himself, eyes closed. "It's not about the article, it is the article."

"I don't understand, the whole city is already talking about the Pre—"

"Don't!" he sighed. "Don't you dare mention that name in my office. This..." he searched for the right word. "Person is a threat to the city. And we do not endorse terrorism. So, we can't publish it."

Staring at the editor, Mpho started chowing on the inside of his cheek.

"Why do you look like that?" he shook his head. "You have that look on your face. Mpho... Don't tell me you posted it online." The editor's gaze went from Mpho's eyes to his lips then his rapidly rising and falling chest. "You didn't."

"Sir..."

The editor raised his hand to Mpho as he turned to his computer, clicking away in needle-dropping silence. An agonizing sigh broke the silence as the editor closed his eyes, pinching the bridge of his nose.

"Sir..."

"Get out."

"I can fix it."

"How can you make sixteen thousand people unread an article? Please tell me cause I'm genuinely intrigued. How can you possibly fix this?"

"Sixteen thousand in one day?" That's a new record for Union Bay City News he thought to himself.

"Get out."

Without a word, Mpho stood and left his supervisor's office. As he returned to his desk, a younger man approached looking rather chipper.

"Bro, your article is blowing up."

"Hayi manje Sizwe."

Mpho sat in front of his computer and sent his fingers flying across the keyboard.

"What are you doing?"

"Taking it down."

"And why would you do that?"

"Because Sizwe, 'we do not endorse terrorism.'"

"Terrorism? Is that what the big man said? Listen to me, he always shouts at me so take my advice. Don't take it down. A criminal was killed, I'd call that justice, a service to the city honestly. Just think about how this will help us?"

"Actually, it may cause more hurt than help," a woman interjected from the adjacent table.

"Jess," Sizwe rolled his eyes.

"He's been the kingpin for so long, he's feared by most, and those who aren't afraid of him still wouldn't challenge him because of public perception. Therefore, his death is likely to create a power vacuum which is not good for us or the police. I'm surprised the war hasn't started yet."

"You're not helping."

"Who said I'm trying to?" The woman got up and patted Mpho on the shoulder. "You messed up Seme," she expressed before walking away. Mpho watched her as she disappeared down the hall.

"So, when are you asking her out?"

"What?"

"Oh, come on, I've seen the way you look at her with that stardust in your eyes Mpho. It's as simple as 'Have dinner with me.' Thank me later," Sizwe backed away making a kissing face.

CHAPTER 8

THE ADVANTAGE OF LIVING 15 minutes away from work was the silent drive home that always gave Mandisa just the right amount of time she needed to cool down and linger on her thoughts. However, today was different for the detective. She was usually irritated by the captain's bickering or her condescending colleagues, but today she resented the fact that she was currently the number one suspect for something she did not do and nothing she said or did would change that. She knew she was told to go home, but instead, she went to the place where she was most unwelcome, the scene of the crime. Unlike last time, she parked her car in reverse in an opening of the forest, changed her shoes and ran to the house through the forest.

OFFICERS BUSTLED AROUND the house. Rushing in wouldn't have been wise, she needed a plan. Then she saw her way in, dressed in the full blue KUPS uniform, blonde hair shining with the help of the sun. James Britz. He was walking into the house with another office. Mandisa pulled her phone out and made the call. It rang a few times before it was answered.

"*Mandisa,*" the voice on the other end of the line whispered.

"I need a favour."

"*You really shouldn't be calling.*"

"I know, but it's important."

"*What is it?*"

"I found something."

"*Something where?*"

"In the house, but I had to leave it inside."

"*What is this thing exactly?*" As he stepped back out of the house, he entered Mandisa's view.

"I can't tell you now, but I need to get it."

"*Fine, what do you need?*"

"I need you to make sure the back door is open, then get everyone out the front."

"*That's not exactly an easy thing.*"

"Find a way." She ended the call. She could see James run his hand through his hair as he returned to the house. Moments later, officers followed him out of the house. She couldn't watch where they were going or why as she knew she had limited time. Finding her way around to the back of the house, she approached the door and slowly stepped in. There were no voices, no footsteps, she was in the clear. She rushed up the stairs, this time in no need to take off her shoes as they were police issued, no way of tracking them back to her. She pulled out a pair of latex gloves, slipped them on and opened the walk-in closet. It was in the same condition she had left it, which meant that her colleagues probably hadn't found it. She opened the drawer, pulled out the velvet tray and placed it aside. With careful delicacy, she grabbed the file folder and stuffed as many documents into it as she could hold, then carried the rest. Wood cricked from a distance. Someone had re-entered the house. Mandisa carefully replaced the tray, slid the drawer closed, slipped out of the closet and closed it.

The footsteps that alerted her of someone's presence were now coming up the stairs.

Mandisa rushed to the window and saw the officers walking towards the house. She had to rush out before they got in, but she had nowhere to go.

The footsteps were getting closer. "Mandisa," a recognizable voice strained to whisper. "Mandisa."

The detective sighed with relief. She stepped out of the room. "James, take this." Mandisa pulled a piece of paper out of the folder, checked it then handed it to James. "Tell them you found it in the closet, there are more in there."

"What closet?"

"There's a walk-in closet in the master bedroom. The door of it is hidden in the wall opposite the window."

"James," a voice called from downstairs.

"Call them up."

"What about you?"

"I'll make it out, just get them all in that room."

"You owe me big time for this."

"And I'll make it up to you, I promise." Mandisa slipped into the bathroom two doors down the hall.

"I'm up here, I think I found something."

Dozens of shoes galloped up the stairs. The detective held her breath as they rushed into the master bedroom.

"What is it?" the voice of Thabiso Simelane.

"I'm not sure exactly, could be a hit list."

"How'd you find this?"

"It was just left in there."

"A secret closet."

"How'd you know this was here?"

Mandisa peeked her head out of the bathroom door. The attention of the officers seemed to have been taken by James' findings as he explained the hollowness of the wall. Mandisa slipped out of the bathroom, tip-toed down the stairs and rushed through the front door and into the thick of the forest. She was only able to catch her breath once she made it to her car. She dropped the folder on the passenger seat and roared the car to life. Her drive was quick but cautious.

WHEN MANDISA GOT HOME, she rushed to her room, leaving the files in the dining room. The diary remained untouched. She opened it and allowed the pen to meet the paper beneath the "I" she had discarded.

I

If the only way for you to trust me is for me to trust you first, there isn't much of an option given the circumstances.

Name your conditions, I accept.

She returned to the dining room with the diary in hand and spread the documents across her dining room table. For a moment she thought she was getting paranoid, but she brushed the feeling off, closed all her curtains, collected her laptop and cell phones and threw them all in the boot of her car before locking her front door – perhaps it was paranoia she thought again. Finally feeling confident that no one could listen or see what she was doing, she sat down to look over the details of the accounts. She knew they wouldn't make all that much sense to her, but she wasn't auditing, she was looking for anything amiss. Even if it wasn't a smoking gun, the smallest mistake still had the potential of shifting her investigation – whether the cartel investigation she was told to stay away from or her new investigation into the Premeditator and the murder of the kingpin, which her enthusiastic colleagues were unlikely to solve any time soon, if ever at all.

"Why would he have these files?" Mandisa thought out loud as she flipped open the file in front of her. How would a criminal like Mkhonto have access to such private documents? She knew Union Bay City Bank, and she knew breaking into the building was no small feat. He had to have used someone on the inside to get the books, someone the bank trusted, someone in management. But who? She threw the thought to the back of her mind as she went through the first document. The account transactions dated from 2005 to 2006. Then another section with less information was dated from the early months of 2012 to the end of the year.

The detective tried to stay away from maths and numbers since high school, but even she could tell something was not adding up with these accounts. The transactions from 2005 to 2006 were assumably those from the city's construction. Many of the transactions were from five private accounts to Union Bay City Bank. This meant the bank was already operating before the city was even opened. The question that haunted Mandisa was "Why not use another already established and well-trusted bank?" What were they hiding, if anything at all? The 2012 transactions were even more complicated than the others. Transactions between the five private accounts, the bank and another new account were scattered throughout the year. The one that confused the detective the most was the one that went from an undisclosed account through Union Bay City Bank to a private account.

What she thought would give her answers had somehow created more questions for her. But maybe she didn't have to answer the questions herself, she thought. Zenzele may be dead, but his family is still very much alive and thriving. Perhaps they knew something. Even if they knew nothing, it couldn't hurt to check.

Mandisa closed the file and wrapped it using the little Christmas gift-wrapping paper she had from last year. After retrieving her devices from the car, she switched on her phone and made a phone call to **Phume (CA)**.

"*Hello,*" a soft voice spoke.

"Phume?"

"*This is she.*"

"It's Mandisa."

"*Xaba?*"

"Do you know any other?"

"*Are you serious? It's been so long,*" the bubbly personality came through the line. "*I lost your number when I switched phones.*"

Mandisa tried to hurry through the formalities and how life had been since they last spoke. "I'm sorry to do this to you, but I need your help."

"*Of course, what's up?*"

She tried to fill Phume in as much as her understanding of the accounts allowed her.

"*Sure, I'll have a look at them, just send a courier, I'll send you my location just now.*"

Having thanked Phume, the detective said goodbye and ended the call. Sure enough, a message pinged Mandisa's phone. She opened it to see the address.

ON HER WAY TO THE MSANI mansion, Mandisa stopped at the courier offices to drop off the gift-wrapped file. Showing her badge, she explained that the contents of the package were highly confidential and that the package needed to be delivered as soon as possible. As she walked back to her car, her phone vibrated in her pocket. She pulled it out and read the name on the screen. **Aunt Zintle.** She stopped in her tracks. It wasn't unusual for her mother's sister to call her. However, the time of the year was unusual for the call. She usually called for occasions that brought the family together, such as Christmas, Easter, or a birthday party for one of her grandparents celebrating an age over eighty. The hoot of a car caught her attention, bringing to her realization that she was standing in the way to the exit of the parking lot.

She lifted her hand to the car in apology and moved out of the way. Reluctantly, she answered her phone, "Malumekazi."

"Mandisa, hello baby, unjani?"

"Ngiyaphila, unjani? Bayaphila ekhaya?"

"No, siyaphila sonke." There was a moment of silence that hung for a while. "Lalela. NgoMgqibelo we're going to see Nontle. I was just wondering if you're going to join us this year. It would be really nice to have you and to see you."

The mention of her mother's name reminded her of the horrifying memory of the last time she saw her alive.

"Mandisa?"

"Yes, sorry," she sighed. "Saturday, I'll see if I can make it."

"Please do nana."

"Okay, can I call you back later malumekazi, I'm still at work okwamanje."

"Okay baby, not a problem."

"Ngiyabonga."

"Okay, bye-bye."

Mandisa considered the offer. Eleven years and she had yet to visit her mother's grave.

CHAPTER 9

KwaZulu Union Bay City, August 11th, 2012

BULLETS FLEW ACROSS the street. Ripping through skin and bone on the hot Saturday morning. Bodies fell in the line of fire as members of rival gangs shot at each other. The war that was fought in the shadows between two crime families had escalated to the point that it went beyond the criminal underworld and onto the streets at the peak the of day. On one side, the ruthless organization of the kingpin known as Mkhonto, who was the man that capitalized the crime of the city, ensuring all crime was fair and monitored under his rule.

Opposite them, was the cunning Myeni clan, who were fighting to dismantle Mkhonto's organization and abolish crime through the means of violence. They were masters of exploitation and they had infiltrated the political offices of the city.

The feud between the two entities was a tale of betrayal and the struggle for power in the city.

Civilians ran in every direction in panic. Nontle Xaba was no exception, pulling her daughter by the wrist, and trying to get to safety. She glanced around as they both hurried along.

A body fell in their way. "Help me."

Nontle hesitated. By profession, she had to help him, but she was a nurse, who worked in a hospital, not a paramedic. She wasn't accustomed to having to help someone on the fly as she had to at that moment. She looked at her daughter, a mere seventeen-year-old. "I'm sorry," she turned away.

"Please," the man grabbed Nontle by the ankle. He winced.

Nontle looked at the man then at her daughter. The teenager's eyes glistened, her breathes quick and tense. "Go."

"Ma..."

"Get in there and stay down," she indicated to the closest building. "Hamba, ndiyeza Mandisa. Hamba Mandisa, I'm right behind you, okay?"

Mandisa released her mother's hand and ran for the building. It took a few moments, but once her daughter was behind safe walls, Nontle got on her knees and assessed the man bleeding at her feet. "You've been shot in the left shoulder, you'll live," she took her scarf off and wrapped it around his shoulder. "What's your name?"

"Steven."

"Okay, Steven, mamela, I need you to let go of the gun, okay?"

The man looked at his hand which still had his firearm in a tight grip. He spread his fingers, allowing the firearm to hit the ground.

"Okay, that's good, now I need you to work with me, can you do that?"

He nodded.

"I'm going to lift you and we'll walk into that building, okay?"

"Yeah."

"Once we're in there, I can get the bullet out of your shoulder and tend to the wound. Okay, let's go." She slung Steven's right arm around her neck and helped him get up. "Come on, work with me."

"I'm trying," he stumbled, trying to find his footing. Together, they hurried towards the building.

"Sisazo fika."

Mandisa held the door open for them. "Come on, come—"

Nontle fell to the ground. Steven followed her fall.

"No!" Mandisa ran out and knelt next to her mother as blood began to stain the back of her shirt. Fighting back tears, Mandisa turned her mother's body around. "Ma."

"Go," she winced. "Go."

"No, I can't. I can't leave you."

"You have to go Mandisa, it's not safe..."

"Ma..." For the first time in her life, Mandisa felt her chest become hollow, a massive wave of fear washing over her.

"Ndiyakuthanda." She grabbed Steven's shirt, "Take... her. Protect..." Her grip lightened, and her head fell to the side as her chest fell and rose no more.

"Ma," Mandisa wept. "Ma..."

Steven forced himself to a hunched position, aware of the ongoing gunfight behind them. "We have to go."

"No..."

"Come on, we have to go," he pulled Mandisa onto his right shoulder and quickly carried her limping into the building she had been hiding in. As soon as he let her down, she pushed him to the ground. He winced, grabbing his shoulder.

"This is your fault," Mandisa yelled. "It's your fault she's... it's your fault."

CHAPTER 10

KwaZulu Union Bay City, November 2nd, 2023

THE REST OF THE DRIVE to the Msani mansion was quiet once the detective shook off the memory. She never really used the radio much and considered it to be more noise than music. As for the informative programs, she considered them negative news. She preferred connecting her phone to the car to listen to playlists of her creation. The silence gave her time to consider everything she had learnt since yesterday and try to guess what hopes she could fish out of the Msani family. However, she knew that she had to be delicate with her approach. Asking for information that only the deceased family member knew wouldn't be easy. Especially considering her current working theory.

The Msani mansion was situated in a posh high-end neighbourhood. It was on the side of the road that had a lake behind the row of houses, a luxury that a few million could afford you in Union Bay. On her first visit, she had compared it to the equivalent of an upper-crust double-story Umhlanga house with an ocean view.

Mandisa didn't call ahead because she couldn't; she had no access to any of the Msani's contact details. However, she knew they would recognize her from Zenzele's case late last year in which she was the lead detective. Or at least she was hoping they would.

The detective hit the buzzer at the gate. "Hello." She waited for a response, but none came. She popped her head out through the window to reveal her face to the well-hidden camera she had missed on her first visit.

To her surprise, the gate swung open allowing her to drive in. The driveway stretched much longer than she remembered and had the width of a two-lane street with a solid line running in the middle which led to a white geometric-shaped fountain. On either side, the garden was well-kept. The mansion walls looked whiter than they were last year, and the windows were as clear as day. She turned into one of the guest parking bays and stepped out of the car. She locked it, and tested the handle, though that was just by habit, not because she needed to where she was.

A stylishly dressed woman much younger than her greeted, "Detective Xaba." She stood at the door with one hand lazily on the frame and the other on her hip.

"Thando," the detective smiled.

"Come in," she stepped aside for Mandisa. "What a surprise."

"A pleasant one, I hope."

"Of course."

"You're answering the door yourself now? What happened to your butler?"

"We fired him," she exaggeratedly exclaimed as she led Mandisa to the living room. "We found out that he was stealing from the wine cellar."

"I'm surprised you'd notice that one out of hundreds of bottles is missing."

"Of course, we'd notice. Those bottles are carefully selected when we buy them."

"And you're sure it was him?"

"I'm joking. It's his day off, we're a family, not a corporation. So contrary to popular belief, we actually treat our employees and guests as they should be." Thando was always vocal about what she believed, both online and offline. And she certainly wasn't afraid of a little controversy every now and again. "With that being said, please, take a seat. Can I get you anything? To drink, to eat?"

"No, I won't be staying long."

Thando nodded as they sat on opposite couches. "This seems serious," Thando remarked.

"It is. I'm sorry to show up unannounced."

"Nonsense, you're always welcome. Not only were you a caring detective, but you kept your word and that means everything to us. However, if you're here to see my mother, you're out of luck. She's still at work. She's spending more time at UB Incorporated than my father did when it was still Union Bay Logistics."

"I can't imagine running one of the biggest companies in the province could be easy. But I wasn't looking for your mother in particular." Mandisa shifted her weight on the couch. "I was hoping you could help me with some... sensitive information."

"Oh-kay?"

"I need you to understand that I wouldn't ask you if I had any other option."

"You're scaring me."

"It's not my intention to. It's about... the group your father was a part of."

Thando's eyes narrowed.

"The Founding Five."

Thando leaned forward, resting her elbows on her knees. "My knowledge about them is limited. But sure. What do you wanna know?"

"Did they ever meet here?"

"No, I don't recall, but then again, I didn't know... I still don't know who they are."

"Your father never mentioned them?"

"My father was a very secretive person," her tone had changed, a hint of irritation. Her words were firm when she spoke. "If he told anyone, it would've been my mother, but even so I doubt he did," she shrugged.

"Have you ever heard him speaking even on the phone with them or about them?"

"Are you asking if I ears dropped on him?"

"I'm asking if he was ever so loud that you happened to overhear him."

Thando sucked a breath through her teeth. "I don't recall ever overhearing him."

"Do you know if he ever kept any private documents in his home office?"

Thando shook her head.

The detective nodded. "Thank you for your time," she got to her feet.

"If you don't mind me asking, is this in connection with that psychopath on the TV or is it about another case?"

"You know I can't talk about active investigations." Mandisa considered her options. She sat back down, "it's about the TV guy. But I could be wrong."

"Or you could be right. What does my father have to do with it? Or the Founding Five."

"I can't tell you that."

"Then I guess I can't help you, detective."

"That's okay," she got up again. "I'll show myself out." The detective made her way to the lobby.

"Wait." She looked up as if trying to mine some information from her brain. "There's a safe."

Mandisa stopped, suppressing a grin. "A safe?" she turned back.

"In his office," she nodded. "It's got a four-digit code. And it needs his fingerprint."

"You're kidding."

"Like I said, he was a secretive man. You can have a look at the safe if you like. But if you want to open it, you'll have to speak to my mother. Only she can give you the go-ahead for that."

"It sounds like you're speaking from experience."

Thando nodded. "I once tried to open it, it's probably needless to say this, but it didn't end well for me. Come on, I'll show it to you."

Thando led the detective into the home office. It was almost still the same as it was when she first stepped into it just over a year ago. A wave of memory washed over her, the corpse on the ground, the note on the table, the shattered glass, spilled whiskey.

"Mandisa? You okay?"

"Yeah," she shook the feeling off. "Where's the safe?"

Thando walked over to a painting hanging over the whiskey table. "Wanna give me a hand?"

Again, Mandisa saw the shattered glass and tasted the spilt whiskey. She shook it off.

Carefully, they took the painting off the wall and leaned it against the table.

Mandisa assessed the safe. It was unlike any she had ever seen before. She pulled her phone out and took a picture of the whole safe, another picture of just the Dial pad and a final picture of the biometric scanner. "I'll speak to your mother as soon as I can, if she allows it, I'll send someone who'll be able to crack the code and retrieve your father's fingerprints."

"How will they do that?"

"He has his ways which I never ask about, plausible deniability."

Thando nodded.

"Once the safe is open, he'll leave. Whatever is inside, take it out and let me know, it might just save lives. You have my number?"

"My brother does, I'll get it from him."

Mandisa shook off a memory before it could completely form at Thando's mention of her brother. "Okay. But this stays between us."

"I understand."

"Ngiyabonga."

"Just happy to help. I hope whatever's in there will be what you're looking for."

"I hope so too."

After replacing the painting, Thando walked the detective out and watched her drive away. Whatever was in that safe had to be a smoking gun. It had to be.

IT WASN'T LONG BEFORE Mandisa arrived at the all-around guarded premises of Union Bay Incorporated. The security guard handed her a tablet and asked her to sign in with her name, ID number, phone number, reason for visit, time of arrival, and her signature. She complied, then drove in, thanking him. The detective noticed that each building had an adjacent parking lot as she drove to the main office building, where she parked on one of the unreserved bays. The air was fresh as she stepped out of the car. She took a moment to take in the astonishing structure before walking into the reception area.

"Good morning, and welcome to Union Bay Incorporated," the receptionist got to her feet. "To whom may I direct you?"

"Nomzamo Msani."

"Your name please."

"Mandisa Xaba."

The receptionist tabbed away at her computer before lifting her head again, "Detective Xaba. She's expecting you, just give me one moment please." She picked up her phone and quickly dialled a number, held the phone to her ear, spoke, waited a moment, and then spoke again before putting the phone down. "She's ready for you. Please take this," she handed Mandisa a thin tablet with a digital interactive map of the enormous Union Bay Incorporated premises zoomed to Mandisa's location. "I have already inserted where Mrs Msani's office is located, all you have to do is follow the arrow," she smiled.

"Thank you." The detective moved away from the reception desk, watching the arrow on the map carefully, she walked in the direction it indicated. Through the beautiful ground floor, up the elevator to the "EXECUTIVE FLOOR". From there, it led her a few steps before the screen displayed:

YOU HAVE ARRIVED

THANK YOU FOR USING *GUIDE ME THERE*

With a light knock, the door swung open.

"Mandisa, come in. I trust you didn't have an issue finding your way."

"Not at all. Thank you for seeing me," she took a seat across from the woman who is now the CEO of one of the biggest companies on the continent. "How are you?"

"I'm good, thank you, yourself?"

"I can't complain. Congratulations on the promotion, it's unfortunate how it came about, but it's certainly a great achievement."

"You get lemons, you make lemonade," Nomzamo waved her guest's concern away. "In any case, if I didn't take this hat, someone else would have. And who knows what vision or agenda that person would be pushing."

"And no one would know Zenzele's vision better than yourself."

"I would certainly hope so. Anyhow, Thando may have given me a heads-up that you're on the way, but she didn't give me any details. So, how could I be of assistance?"

The detective glanced at the door a moment, then turned back to Nomzamo, her smile fading.

The CEO pushed a button under her desk and the office door closed.

"I shouldn't be sharing this with you so if anyone asks, I didn't."

Nomzamo nodded.

"There's currently an active investigation into the Founding Five. Which means Zenzele and all those who were involved may be revealed through the course of this week or month. I'm sorry to have to touch a healing wound, but I need your help. It's to my knowledge that your husband had a safe."

"To your knowledge?"

"It would certainly make sense for him to want to keep some things close to the chest."

"And how does this safe come into play with your investigation exactly?"

"I need to know what's inside. If there's a chance that it could be helpful to the investigation, then I need to know."

"What my husband kept to himself was his business."

"I understand."

"I'm sure you do, but you don't really care, do you? You're just here as a mere formality. You were going to open that safe with or without my consent, isn't that how y'all operate? You do whatever you like as long as it helps the investigation?"

"It shouldn't be that way."

"But it is. Where were you when your colleagues were digging through my past, rampaging my house, just because I became CEO? Where were you when they didn't want the will to be carried out just because of the circumstances of Zenzele's death? Where were you?"

The detective bowed her head.

"We needed you and you weren't there. The only reason I'll let you open that safe is because I want to know what's inside. Now unfortunately, I'm not privy to sitting around and waiting, so when the safe is open, you will go through everything with Thando."

"That's unorthodox."

"Take it or leave it."

CHAPTER 11

JUST AFTER LUNCHTIME, the activities had decreased at Union Bay City News. Everyone busied themselves with their work, glued behind their computer screens. Mpho was no exception. He had spent about half an hour scrolling through the comments people wrote about his article.

'It's concerning to know that someone killed the most gangster person in town. Was it a power move by another criminal entity or was it just a concerned citizen doing what the police can't?'

'Where is the justice?'

'I never said this but, he got what was coming to him. At least our streets will be safer now.'

'When a cop kills a civilian, you call it police brutality. But when a civilian kills a criminal, y'all call it manslaughter? As far as I'm concerned, it's called justice.' Mpho had the feeling that one was from Sizwe.

'They still haven't found him? What are the police doing?'

'Sitting on their hands as usual, LOL' was one of the replies to the previous comment.

'So you're all really in support of this vigilante? What happens if he decides he wants to start killing innocent people?'

That particular comment caught Mpho off-guard. Forcing him to wonder what would happen to his daughter if he was killed. He had to be more careful. Perhaps his supervisor was right. He was so zoned out that he couldn't see his colleagues flooding to one side of the office, but he could hear the voices fighting to be heard over the noise that filled the room.

"Someone turn up the volume on the TV!" someone shouted.

"Where's the remote?" another replied.

Mpho got up from his seat when he realized that everyone had their attention on the television hanging from the front of the bullpen.

The editor had pushed his way to the front of the crowd, yelling over everyone else to quieten down just as the UBNL emergency broadcast alert faded to black. The editor raised the volume on the side of the television. The sound of footsteps and slow clapping echoed through. Returning in his full black three-piece suit, hat and balaclava, the man dubbed the Premeditator began. "Congratulations. You solved the first riddle. But with the end of one chapter is the start of another."

"What do you want from us?" yelled a man in the crowd. The editor shushed him.

"I sometimes tell the truth, and sometimes lie. Many hate me, but many more love me. I can be the key to freedom or to prison. I sometimes win, and sometimes lose but I'm never at risk when I play, what am I?"

"A murderer!" the voice yelled out again.

"Get out," the editor instructed.

"Solve the riddle and save a life, this time, it is in your best interest to think fast and act faster. You have five hours." And with that, the screen faded to black.

As if priorly rehearsed, everyone turned to Mpho, their faces waiting for some kind of answer. Which never came. Instead, he bolted out like he had a plane to catch. Everyone watched him, some attempted to follow him.

"Hey, hey, hey, don't even think about it," yelled the editor. "Get back to work." He watched everyone linger a bit. "Now!"

DOWN THE STREET THE journalist went, racing past the traffic, only to stop when he reached the edge of the bay. It was the only place he felt at peace. The only place his investigations didn't matter. The only place his investigations didn't matter. The only place in the city where no one could care less who he was. With his hands on his knees, his breathing only got heavy by the second. Then as he opened his eyes, he noticed another pair of feet next to his. Black shoes and black pants.

When the person spoke, the voice was soft but firm. "You shouldn't have written that article."

CHAPTER 12

AS THE EYES OF THE journalist travelled up the body occupying the space next to him, he noticed a black t-shirt. The pounding of his heart was up to his throat as he continued up the body of the person who rested their arms on the railing. Reaching the head of the body, a cold chill tremored his spine making the air seem like breathing evaporating ice.

"Hlisa umoya," the voice continued. "I just want to talk."

Then as the body shifted its weight, the journalist could finally identify – partially – the person who caught him by surprise. "You're a cop," he sighed, relief washing over him.

"I know," Mandisa replied, her gaze never leaving the mass of water on the other side of the railing.

"You were there that night, I saw you."

"Yes, and you made things quite difficult for me."

"Di- difficult? Define please."

"Bunga fanelanga uba pha."

"I was doing my job."

"Your job puts people at risk."

"What people?"

"Yourself for one. Your daughter."

"Don't talk about my daughter," he shifted closer to Mandisa, now looking her in the eyes.

"Did you even stop to think that this so-called Premeditator could be a serial killer?"

"He certainly doesn't speak like one."

"And how do serial killers speak?"

"Not like him."

Mandisa shook her head. "So awuwazi."

"And you do?"

"Yes. Because it's my job to know."

Realizing how close they were, Mpho took a step back. "You said you want to talk. So?"

The detective turned back to the mass of water. "I can't trust anyone at my station. Therefore, I don't think I can trust anyone at any of the other stations. Which means you're going to help me ensure the three people left stay alive."

"What makes you think there's three people left?"

"I have a theory."

"That theory being?"

"I can't tell you right now."

"Why not?"

"Because you're a journalist."

"So why would I help you?"

"Because you've proven that you're willing to risk everything."

"And how do I know you're not the Premeditator?"

"You can't know that, now can you?"

"Exactly."

"But I'm not."

"It's not like you'd say you are if you were."

"Does your daughter know that one day she could be waiting to be picked up from school, but daddy doesn't show up?"

"Are you threatening me?"

"Merely asking if she understands your choice of career. It wasn't wise to pursue this knowing you have something to lose. Someone to lose."

"Don't you have someone to lose?"

Mandisa's mind jumped back to her aunt's offer to visit her mother's grave. "How familiar are you with Vihaan Naicker?"

"You're changing the subject."

"It's either you can help me, or you can't. And if awukwazi, I'll find someone else who will."

Mpho sighed as he rested his arms against the railing. "He's the owner of the biggest bank in the city, so I'd say I'm not very familiar with him."

"You've written an article about his bank."

"That was a long time ago." He tilted his head to look at the detective. "Do you think he's the next target?"

"Andiyazi. But if I knew, I wouldn't tell you."

"Let me guess, because you can't talk about ongoing investigations?"

"Because it's too dangerous for you to know. It's better to limit risk."

"So only you know? You realise how that makes you look, right?"

"We need to have a word with him."

"You're changing the subject again. But by 'we' you mean you."

"I mean you."

"Excuse me?"

"You're a journalist, you know how to butter people. Whereas I'm a cop, people lock up when they see me."

"What makes you think he could be a target?"

"It would be pretty hard to build anything without money. You need to talk to him and find out what he knows about the financing of this city's creation."

"He doesn't match the description of the riddle though."

"What riddle?"

"Th- the new one. Didn't you hear it?"

"Hayi."

"Then—"

"What's the riddle?"

"Okay, it's uhm…" he closed his eyes to raddle his brain for the riddle. "Okay, 'I sometimes tell the truth, and sometimes lie. Many hate me, but many more love me. I can be the key to freedom or to prison. I sometimes win, and sometimes lose but…' ah. 'But I'm never at risk when I play, what am I?'"

"Truth, lie, hate, love, freedom, prison. Win, lose, risk, play." Mandisa numbered with her fingers as she spoke, "Truth, lie, freedom, prison, win, lose. The answer is lawyer."

"W—what? Just like that?"

"Masambe."

"To where?"

"The bank. You have to find out who the lawyer is."

"How?"

"You'll figure it out."

"And if I don't?"

"It wouldn't be wise to gamble against someone with nothing to lose."

Mpho immediately followed the detective as she headed to her car.

CHAPTER 13

UNION BAY CITY BANK. The city's first and yet to be dethroned biggest bank. The structure of which was an architectural wonder in itself. A seemingly large geometric glass building consisting of four structures of varying numbers of floors. However, from above it spelt out UBCB. A rather unnecessary thing to have done the journalist recalled as he entered the bank. Having called on the way to request a meeting, Mpho was warmly welcomed by the receptionist, and asked to wait a few minutes while "Mr Naicker finished a meeting with a client."

As he waited in the seating area, Mpho was offered a variety of hot beverages, which he politely declined. The building's interior was quite modern considering it was a decade and a half old he thought to himself. Everything was either white or shiny – as if daily polished, including the white leather couch he was fearful of sitting on.

"Mr Seme," the CEO greeted, holding his hand out to Mpho. "I hope I haven't kept you waiting too long."

Quickly rising, he responded, "No, not at all. Thank you for your time."

As Vihaan led the journalist to the elevator, he instructed for the bank's cafeteria barista to send two coffees to his office as soon as possible. They stepped into the glass-floored elevator.

"Is it too late to mention that I have a phobia of elevators?" Mpho glanced down as they were lifted from the ground.

"You have nothing to worry about, one second you're stepping in. And the next, you're stepping out," the elevator dinged and slid open.

The CEO led the way to his office. "Please take a seat," he began as he got comfortable across the table from his guest. "Mpho Seme of Union Bay City News. I read your article about the Premeditator. It was... daring to say the least. In fact, I often read articles from your newspaper. They're often interesting."

"Thank you sir."

"Please call me Vihaan. My kids call me sir. I don't believe this is our first meeting."

"No, it's not."

"How may I help?"

"Right, uhm... A few years ago, I wrote an article about the bank, I'm not sure if you remember it."

"Remember it? I can't forget it," he indicated to one of the articles framed on the wall behind him. "You didn't hear this from me, but that was the best article I've ever read. And I'm not just saying that because it's about my bank," he chuckled.

"I'm glad you enjoyed it, I'm actually following up on it... sorry, I forgot to ask, would you mind if I recorded this session?"

"Not at all."

Mpho pulled his phone out and called the first number on his call log – which silently rang for just over a second before being answered. He locked his phone and placed its screen down on the table. "Right, as I was saying... A few years ago, I wrote an article about Union Bay City Bank. Can you tell me how the bank has changed, if it has, from then till now?"

Vihaan leaned back in his chair, "Well..." He began, explaining the improved technology that they're now using, the investments they're making into the city, and the university students they're funding.

"Those are quite the achievements, and congratulations on remaining in the top 10 banks in Africa."

"All thanks go to the team we have here. We are a community, no, a family. Except if we give you money, we do expect it back," he chuckled.

"I believe in the last interview we had... you explained to me that this bank was established..." he pulled out his small notepad, flipped through it, and pretended to be reading through some notes, "on the... same month as the city, is that correct?"

"Yes, that's right."

"So can I assume that this bank had a hand in helping build the city?"

Vihaan looked at the journalist, considering. Mpho knew that his interviewee was trying to read him, so he put on his poker face and waited for an answer. "We helped just as much as anyone else did," Vihaan finally replied with less enthusiasm.

"Well, I thought that maybe you may," his voice now just more than a whisper, "off the record, know a little more than we do about the financing of the city."

Vihaan turned away, squinting his eyes at the window. When he returned his gaze to Mpho, his jar was tight, his eyes burning.

From his few years of interviewing people, Mpho could identify that something in the CEO had split causing an internal war.

"After the city was opened. I became Zenzele Msani's banker and as a result, he brought in a lot of business for us," he sighed. "That's how UBCB got to be what it is today."

Vihaan regained his composure as the door opened, revealing a young man carrying a tray of two coffees. After placing the cups on the table, the man excused himself and closed the door as he left.

"Zenzele Msani? So, you worked with the Founding Five."

"I wouldn't say I worked with them. Zenzele was very... private about them. It wasn't exactly a topic he wanted to publicly discuss."

"But he did speak about them in private?"

"I think I've told you enough. The Founding Five fought so you could live the lifestyle you live. You should appreciate that and stop asking questions no one has answers to." He glanced at his watch and then looked back at the journalist. "It seems our time is up." "It seems our time is up."

"Thank you for your time," he picked up his cell phone and ended the call. "Have a nice day." He smiled at Vihaan before walking out and returning downstairs, where Mandisa was waiting in her car.

"I'm sorry I couldn't get enough answers."

"On the contrary," Mandisa responded, with her eyes still glued to her laptop screen, rewinding to repeatedly listen to a single line.

"The Founding Five fought," "The Founding Five fought," "The Founding Five fought so you could live the lifestyle you live. You should appreciate that and stop asking questions no one has answers to."

She paused the recording. "Mthandazo Makhanya."

"Who's that?"

"He was the lead lawyer who fought for the independence of Union Bay. Without him, this wouldn't be a city-state."

"Someone paid attention in history."

"You ever been to Durban?"

"No."

"You're gonna wanna put your seatbelt on."

CHAPTER 14

ANY GLOBAL POSITIONING System would've told you that it takes close to three hours to drive from KwaZulu Union Bay City to Durban. Taxi drivers would've told you two and a half hours. Mandisa seemed to prove both of those estimations inaccurate. But then again, the speed cameras caught her like a paparazzo. Most of the drive was quiet, except Mpho trying to start a conversation every so often. Mandisa gave him short one-word and at times two-word answers.

"What's with the diary?" Mpho reached for the thin book on the dashboard.

The detective stomped on the brake, released it then hit the accelerator again, causing Mpho to jolt forward and then back hard onto the seat.

"It's none of your business."

"Well, I'm sorry," he stole a glance at Mandisa. "I didn't mean to pry." A few uncomfortable moments passed before he felt the urge to break the silence. "By the harbour," he stole a quick glance at Mandisa, "you said... you've got nothing to lose."

"Did I?"

"You insinuated it. What did you mean?"

"I need you to understand something. I'm not just another person you're trying to interview, so what you're doing, trying to make conversation and asking questions, stop it."

Mpho visibly shrunk in his seat.

The detective sighed. "You want to talk so much, here's a question for you. Why did you become a journalist?"

Mpho hesitated. "Well... I didn't exactly choose to be a journalist."

"Don't tell me it chose you."

"Then I won't tell you." Mpho scratched his head. "I was born into a family of overachievers; I grew up around them. Doctors, businessmen and women, lawyers, and even politicians. You can imagine the expectation."

I really can't, Mandisa thought of saying. She glanced at the journalist then refocused on the road.

"I didn't know what to do after high school, so I studied law."

"Because that's easy?"

"Cause it was better than becoming a politician."

"So are eighty per cent of other professions." Mpho didn't respond. "Why law?"

"It's what my mother wanted to do. But she couldn't because she left school when she was about sixteen or seventeen, the details get fuzzy."

The car slowed a little as Mandisa thought back to that period of her life.

"She had to take care of her brothers and sisters after the incident. We don't talk about it. But in any case, it didn't help that I chose law because after five years as a lawyer, I became an investigative journalist, my family wasn't pleased, to say the least."

"Don't take this the wrong way but you would've made a horrible lawyer."

"Why would you say that?"

"I feel like this is not something I have to tell you, but you talk too much."

"Lawyers literally get paid to talk."

"Yes, but not as much as you do. No offense."

"Some taken."

"What I'm trying to say is that the more you talk, the more likely you are to slip up." She could see the journalist nod. "You saved a lot of people trouble by changing professions."

Mpho chuckled and shook his head.

"You're a good journalist, no matter what your family may say about you."

"Thanks. Can I ask you a question?"

"No," Mandisa replied.

"How do you know Durban so well?"

The detective sighed.

"I answered your question. It's only fair that you answer mine."

"You think I care about what's fair?" she glanced at the journalist for a moment.

"No, but you may still need my help, and there's still a long drive back we'll have, so to avoid that being awkward, it would make sense that you answer."

"I was born and raised here."

"You're a Durbanite?" Mpho's voice peaked. "Sorry, I've just heard people use that term before. Why'd you move? If you don't mind me asking, did something happen?"

"The hospital my mother was working for at the time shut down, so she lost her job, along with hundreds of other people. Sick patients suddenly had to find another hospital or wait to die because the government suddenly didn't have the funds to keep running a place where people are supposed to get help."

"What about your father?"

"The man I no longer consider my father, he lost his humanity when I was seventeen."

"What do you mean?"

"He spent most of his time with a bottle in his hand or beating... he was abusive."

Mpho shifted a bit uncomfortably in his seat. He adjusted the seatbelt as if it was affecting his breathing. "I'm sorry."

"Don't be. It's not your fault. Life deals you cards, and you have to play the best hand. It's just how it is."

"So, after the hospital shut down, you moved to Union Bay, city of innovation. I'm sure your mom got a job and is now working as one of the best doctors at Mncwango Med or one of those other private hospitals."

"She was a nurse."

His journalism instincts kicking in, Mpho recognized the dent of sorrow in Mandisa's voice when she said, "was". "Oh, uhm... I'm so—"

"We're here." Mandisa pulled into a parking bay outside a skyscraper. Her hands were still on the wheel, her vision fading into the distance.

"Are you okay?" Mpho turned to face Mandisa. "If you want, I could speak to him on my own."

"Stay here," the detective instructed as she stepped out of the car.

"Wait, don't you need my help?"

"No."

"Then why'd you bring me among?"

"I didn't, you chose to accompany me." After entering the building, she had to sign in at the two-manned security station, where they gave her a visitor tag for the floor she was going to. The twenty-first floor. Because lawyers had to have a great view she thought to herself. Or at least from the law-based series she enjoyed watching it seemed that way. She quickly moved passed the offices. She knew the Founding Partners had the corner offices; the challenge was which one of the four corners was Mthandazo's. To avoid walking in circles, she stopped at the office of someone who seemed less busy than everyone else and knocked on the open door.

The woman looked up from her phone screen and waved Mandisa in. "Hi."

"Hi," she pasted on her well-practised smile from all her undercover work. "I hope you can help me. I'm looking for Mthandazo Makhanya's office."

"End of the hall, corner officer." She indicated towards the left.

"Thank you." The detective hurried in the direction she was pointed towards and found the office. It was much bigger than the rest.

"Can I help you?" a woman asked from a desk outside the office.

With a flash of her badge to the Founding Partner's secretary, Mandisa let herself into the glass office.

"You can't—" she got up to follow Mandisa, her heels not allowing her to catch up. "You're not allowed in there."

"...Direction that she wants to go with this case, then I can bring in tree law and she'll end up paying three times the amount I'm offering right now," the lawyer concluded to the person on the other side of his call as he turned to his entering guest. After a few moments of listening to the response, he continued, "Yeah, and the next time you call, it better be to tell me that she's accepted." And with that, he put his phone down. "I wasn't aware that I had a meeting."

"I wasn't aware I had to make one," she flashed her badge before returning it to the comfort of her jacket.

"I'm sorry sir, she just let herself in, I tried to stop her," the secretary explained.

"It's okay, close the door please." He watched as his secretary closed the door and retreated to her desk. "If that badge is legitimate and any indication, you seem to be far out of your jurisdiction, detective."

"You don't even know why I'm here, and you're already getting defensive."

"How may I help you?" he sighed.

"You can start by stepping away from the window."

"And why should I do that?"

"Because it's in your best interest to follow my instructions."

"In my best—you do realize you're talking to a lawyer? So, until you tell me exactly what's going on, I'm not going anywhere with you."

"I'm not asking you to go anywhere with me, I'm asking you to step away from the window. There's a possibility that your life is in danger."

"I'm a lawyer, my life is always in danger."

"This is not a joke Mr Makhanya. Someone is trying and so far succeeding in erasing the Founding Five of Union Bay City from existence and I need you to tell me why."

"The Founding Five," he scoffed. "I haven't heard that in years. But in any case, that's all behind me now. I want nothing to do with those people. Take it from me, nothing good comes from them. And as you can see, I've moved on and moved up with life."

"Well clearly someone else hasn't 'moved on and moved up', so do you want to tell me what the five of you did?"

"There's a lot we did," he sunk into his chair. "Some things good... others not so. But there's nothing I can tell you; Zenzele made us all sign an NDA."

"So, you were a part of the Founding Five?"

The lawyer froze for a moment. "You didn't know, did you?"

"I had a hunch, you just confirmed it."

"Yeah," Mthandazo sighed. "But like I said, I signed a non-disclosure."

"Then tell me who the other two are," she demanded.

"I don't know," he shrugged. "Zenzele made sure there were no names, no faces, no IDs, no trace of who we are. That man," he shook his head, his eyes getting a shade redder. "He had a lot of secrets, and a lot more lies."

"You say that like you don't."

"Am I being charged with anything?" He stood, regaining his confidence.

"Not yet," she responded, staring daggers at Mthandazo, who returned the same gaze.

For a moment, the computer stopped humming, the clock stopped ticking and everything seemed to be still. Then a rattle of glass broke the tension.

"I told you to stay in the car," the detective shouted as she saw Mpho.

"We were wrong," the journalist panted. It was Nozizwe Biyela... she was the next target. We ran out of time," Mpho explained between breaths.

"So, she's... dead?" the lawyer asked.

"Yeah," Mpho nodded.

With a sigh, the detective started massaging her forehead.

"That's the second person."

The landline started ringing. Mthandazo looked at the phone and then at the detective. "Can I take this?"

"Yeah," Mandisa slumped into a chair.

"Mthandazo Makhanya. Hello?" Confused he looked up to Mandisa. "It's for you," he offered the phone.

Hesitantly, Mandisa accepted it, her eyes remaining on Mthandazo.

"*Hello detective,*" a voice called through the phone.

"Who is this?" she turned to one of the windows, scanning the surrounding buildings for a hiding point.

"*You and I have so much that we must discuss. Please do me a favour and tell those two liars by profession to get out. Unless you want me to add them to my list.*"

"Can I have the room," she requested keeping her gaze on the city.

Though, agitated, the lawyer complied. Mpho followed suit behind him.

"*Please don't think about calling your friends back at the station to have them track the call.*"

"I don't have friends at work. I have colleagues and that's all they are."

"*Hmm, wise. You may know me as the Premeditator. A name I did not like at first, but I think it's growing on me.*"

"Do you have another name I can call you?"

"*Not particularly, no. However, I do suppose you could call me the broker, if you must.*"

"Okay broker, would you like to tell me what the people you're killing did to you?"

"*Oh, careful detective, you're insinuating that they deserve what's happening to them.*"

"You're not answering my question."

"*Yes. I have to say I'm disappointed that you went for the wrong person though you got the riddle correct. You just can't trust lawyers these days, am I right?*"

"I take it you called me for a reason beyond gloating."

"*Yes. A riddle.*"

"You had to call me for it?"

"*I did. You and I have been working well together thus far.*"

"Let's get one thing straight, I don't work with murderers."

"*Are you sure about that? Did you know that the police probably kill, on average, more people a year than any criminal entity ever could?*"

"Emphasis on probably."

"*And they call that enforcing the law.*"

The detective moved to the other window. "You said you have a riddle for me."

"*For the love of money is the root of all evil. Can't live without me, nor can you trust me. Many have trusted me, though they don't know me. I'm a person of my word, however, it fluctuates. I'm strict with rules and I mind the smallest details, what am I?*"

Mandisa glanced over her shoulder, then looked back over the cityscape. "I don't know."

"*Oh, that's disappointing. Well, let's hope you figure it out detective because you're the only one I've told the riddle to.*"

"Why?"

"*Do you even need to ask? We make a great team.*"

"We're not a team."

"I suppose it does depend on who's asking. I do hope it's true what they say about the third time being the charm. You have thirty-six hours. And tell the journalist to call me."

"How would he do that?"

"He will receive an email with the instructions. Oh, and I wouldn't tell the captain about our little talk."

The line goes dead just as Mandisa's phone starts ringing. Frustrated, she answered, "Captain."

"Xaba, where are you?"

"Out of town."

"You seemed to have chosen quite a convenient time to disappear."

"With all due respect sir, you told me to cool off, so what are you talking about?"

"Get to the station right now, we need all hands on deck."

"What happened?"

"You'll be debriefed at the station."

"Yes sir," she replied through gritted teeth.

CHAPTER 15

POLICE PERSONNEL BUSTLED on the Biyela & Co. floor of the massive office building, working through Nozizwe Biyela's office. Or at least what remained of it. Furniture flipped. Books and paperwork scattered across the floor. And her body meticulously placed on her chair in front of the blood-painted window. The red liquid now dry on the giant glass window spelt out three words: "YOU WERE WARNED!" The office was filled with police officers and CSI's bustling back and forth, trafficking among themselves. And at the centre of it all stood the captain as he lowered his phone from his ear. Next to him was Detective Simelane.

"Mandisa is going to head back to the station. As soon as she arrives, I want you to keep her there. Make sure she doesn't leave, she doesn't snoop around, but also make sure she doesn't get suspicious 'cause you know how she can get," the captain instructed. "Is that clear?"

"Yes sir," Thabiso responded before leading a group of officers out, barking orders to them.

Turning back to the body and the CSI working around it, Sithole asked, "Okay, please explain to me what we have one more time."

"A real statement," the young CSI responded without turning his attention away from the body. "Looks like she died because of the cuts to her wrists, bled out in minutes. There are some markings below and above her lips indicating that her mouth was taped shut during the murder. If you look closely at her wrists, you can see that she was tied during some of the process, however, I can't tell if the rope was untied before or after her wrists were cut, that much I can only confirm once we get her body in the lab."

"Anything on her neck?"

"Yes, I was about to get to that. She was strangled right around her neck," he lifted his hands to illustrate. "Assailant used both hands, which could mean they have small hands, which then means it could actually be a female, rather than a man."

"Male."

"Sorry?"

"Male, not man. Men don't treat women like this."

"Right. Anyway, as for indications that she fought back against her attacker. None from what I can tell at the moment. Which leads me to think that the mess of paperwork was done after she died rather than being a result of struggling."

"But why?"

"Maybe, there's something the attacker was looking for. But there's no way of knowing for sure so that much I can't tell you."

"Time of death?"

"We'll know once the autopsy is in."

Sithole finally considered the possibility of the theory Detective Simelane was building upon. He had to ask himself if Mandisa could really be behind these two major murders. She certainly has the skillset. But as to what could be the reason that pushed her over the edge, Sithole could only wonder. "But what you are telling me is that there's a possibility that the most dangerous criminal in the city was killed by a woman?"

"No, I'm saying you shouldn't rule out that possibility until we have enough info to know for sure."

"Well, is there a possibility that this was a two-person job?"

"Definitely." The CSI started packing his gear. "What makes things even trickier is that this person could be very crazy and perhaps require some serious help."

"Or?"

"Or they're highly intelligent, and just mocking us."

"That doesn't exactly boost my confidence Khumalo. Tell me something I can say to the press."

"Run," the CSI sighed.

"That's not funny."

"I'm not tryna be sir. But this person we're dealing with. I don't think we've ever faced anyone like this before. He or she is too detail-orientated to be a random serial killer and too involved to be a hitman." He finally stood to meet the captain's eyes. "He or she is not afraid to attack someone in their own home or their place of work in broad daylight, and they're not shy of the public eye either. That makes them very dangerous in my opinion," the CSI concluded. "Whatever you decide to say to the press, be very careful. People are still a little tense."

With a quick glance at the decaying body, Sithole headed to the entrance of the building to address the growing crowd of curious bystanders and journalists. As soon as the captain stepped through the door, a wave of questions washed over him. "Okay, okay, calm down," he yelled over the voices of the restless crowd. "Let us not speculate, assume, or jump into any conclusions," he began. "Firstly, you need to understand that as of this moment, you know as much as I do. Perhaps a little less but the point is it's not much. Which brings me to my second point, this building is a public place, and whoever came in or went out would have been seen or caught on camera. However, with that said, we would really appreciate it if anyone who was here over the weekend and might have seen any suspicious activity came forward and informed me or any other police official."

"So, the time of death was during the weekend?" a voice in the crowd yelled.

"Nothing has been set in stone yet so we're keeping our options open."

"Captain Sithole, can you confirm that Miss Biyela's death was part of what the Premeditator has, quote, 'planned' for the city?"

"I cannot comment on that as it is still an ongoing investigation, and I will not be taking any more questions. I plead with all the people of our city to be vigilant and stay safe. Thank you."

Before he could hear another question, the captain walked away from the crowd surrounded by his officers.

CHAPTER 16

HAVING RETURNED TO the station, Detective Simelane ran up the stairs with his officers hot on his heels. Stepping through the doors, their boots announced their presence.

"Njabulo, Aryan, James, my office now," he continued through the station. He opened the door to the office he shared with Jabu.

The detective looked up from his paperwork. The expression on his partner's face was focused, his arms folded over his chest. "That bad?"

"I'll tell you just now, let's just wait for the gents."

As instructed, the members of the KUB City Strike Team group filtered into the office, James closing the door after stepping in.

"I'm sure you're all aware that we were just at Biyela & Co., and I can confirm that the, what do they call it, something partner..."

"Founding," one of the officers who were with him assisted.

"Yes, founding partner, Nozizwe Biyela was indeed killed, in her office, and it seems like it may have happened over the weekend."

"The weekend?"

"Yeah, according to Sithole, there's a possibility."

"Hmm."

"Premeditator?"

"Considering that the style doesn't match how Mkhonto was killed that's still unclear, but likely."

"Lo mfana unesbindi."

"Cha."

"Cha?"

"There's a chance that... uSithole just called me njengoba sibuya with an update. According to Khumalo, the CSI, not the other one, there's a possibility that it was a woman."

"Umfazi?"

"Jabu and I hadn't ruled that possibility out from the get-go," he glanced at his partner. "We were considering that it could actually be one of our own."

"What do you mean?"

"Mandisa," Jabu answered.

James glanced from Jabu to Thabiso but remained silent.

"That's a massive accusation," Njabulo remarked. "We have to have solid proof before something like that can be taken to Sithole."

"Sithole knows where we stand."

"I hoped we're wrong," Thabiso began again. "But things aren't looking good for Xaba. Caught on the scene of the crime last night, and today she's nowhere to be found."

"Okay, I'm sorry, I've just been quiet trying to understand all of this," James brushed his stubbled beard. "So, in movies, there's something called a plot hole, so it's when something very questionable happens and it's not addressed. In franchise films they try to address them in sequels etc, but in reality, we don't have those so if the plot hole isn't addressed, there's—"

"Get to the point James."

"Sorry, uhm... The 'Premeditator' only introduced him or herself yesterday. But you say Nozizwe was killed over the weekend. It's Thursday now. I'm not a filmmaker myself, but that's a massive plot hole."

"That just means it's possible that it wasn't the Premeditator."

"But now that would mean there's a body out there we haven't found."

The tension in the room finally became tangible as the officers looked at each other considering the possibilities.

"The weekend thing is just a possibility, Sithole could be wrong, but we'll know for sure once the autopsy is in. James, have you made any progress with the documents?"

"Nothing worth reporting, but I'm still on top of it."

"We need something tangible before end of day," said Jabu.

"We're getting nowhere right now. Aryan, help James with what he's looking into. Jabu, take a small team to Nozizwe's house, there should be something that hints at why she was the target. The rest of you go back to Mkhonto's place and find everything we missed. I have to stay here and wait for Xaba's arrival. Let's go."

CHAPTER 17

DURING THE LONG DRIVE back to KwaZulu Union Bay City, an argument broke out between the detective and the journalist about what should be done. Mpho wanted to work with the police and explain everything to them. But Mandisa was against the idea and detested it. By the time they got back into the city, the tension in the car was thick. The detective knew sharing some of what the Premeditator had told her with Mpho would be risky. But she never could've guessed how he would want to handle the situation.

"Lalela, I have to take care of this myself," Mandisa argued.

"No, you don't. You're not even on the case."

Mandisa turned to the journalist, her jaw clenching.

"What, you think I don't know a rogue cop when I see one? Detective Simelane was given this case for him to figure out."

"You don't know what you're talking about."

"I know exactly what I'm talking about. I have connections everywhere Mandisa, almost no piece of news in the city passes me. We have to walk into the station and tell them everything."

"You can do that on your own."

As the car pulled to a stop, the journalist took a look out his window. His eyes blocked welling tears like a dam wall.

"This is you," Mandisa sighed.

"Mandisa think about this. This is not a decision to be taken lightly, it's one there's no coming back from. We can still—"

"Get out," the detective disturbed him. "There is no we, you made that clear."

Mpho opened his door and jumped out of the car.

"This is a bad idea and you're going to regret it, but I wish you all the best," said Mandisa.

"Yeah, you too," Mpho closed the door. Taking a step back, he sighed as he watched the car speed off. With a deep breath, he walked up the stairs of the police station and entered to find it bustling with activity. Mpho walked up to a counter to address the resting officer.

However, the officer jolted up from his seat as if recognizing the journalist and shouted, "Hayi, hayi, no comment."

"Wait."

"No comment."

"You don't understand, I need to see the captain," Mpho tried to explain.

"No... comment," the officer repeated. "Now if you'll excuse me, there's a growing line behind you."

"It's about the Premeditator!"

The many people in the station would tell you different stories of what followed the journalist's shout. Mpho, however, recalled it in three steps. The first was needle-dropping silence, then being escorted into an interrogation room, followed by the captain sitting square in front of him with a gaze intense enough to burn a hole through one's soul.

"Mpho Seme," Sithole began. "I've been told that you wanted to see me. Your article that you wrote has created quite a negative stir for me. So please listen to me very carefully. I don't have time for you to waste today, okay? So if you have some credible information for me, start talking, otherwise, get out of my station."

Returning to his senses Mpho began his recollection of the truth with a twisted version of it, "He called me."

"The Premeditator?" Thabiso questioned.

Mpho looked up at Thabiso, who was standing next to the captain. "Yes. He called." He was careful not to directly say the Premeditator called me.

"And said what?"

"Hold on," the captain interrupted. "How do we know we can trust you?"

Recalling Mandisa's hesitation of working with her colleagues, the wheels started turning in the journalist's head. "I don't suppose you know who the killer is. If you did, you would've caught him by now. Which means you need all the help you can get and right now, I think we both know I'm that help. Meaning trusting each other doesn't matter as much as catching this murderer. That is unless you enjoy the publicity your station is receiving right now Captain. But if the words of the minister are any indication, I don't think you should be. So, with all due respect, I think you'll want to hear what I have to say, in fact, I think you need me, because at the moment, your best detective has gone rogue because of your lack of trust, and she's done a lot more than the rest of your officers have combined. Now I may not know you that well, but from what I've gathered, you suffer from an inferiority complex, and all your officers know it. But none of them seem to have the gumption to say it to your face," he concluded now jittery and high on adrenaline and a bit of anxiety.

"You got some nerve."

"This is a serious matter and a threat to city security. And for that reason, I believe it should be treated as such," Mpho explained, wildly blinking and no longer able to maintain eye contact. "Sir."

Infuriated, the Captain asked, "What did he say to you?"

"The Premeditator?" Mpho asked antsy.

"Yes. The Premeditator, what did he say?"

"Not much. Said that in thirty-six hours he'll strike again."

"Thirty-six hours from when?" Thabiso asked.

"About three, four, maybe five hours at most ago."

The captain pinched the bridge of his nose as he sighed.

"So, thirty-one hours."

"What was the riddle?" asked Sithole.

"I don't know."

"What do you mean you don't know?"

"He didn't tell me anything." The most honest thing Mpho had said since he entered the station.

"You just said—"

"That's enough!" Sithole interrupted. "Do you have his number?"

"I have an email from him. It has his details," he pulled his phone out.

"You've been referring to the Premeditator as he and him a lot now, how do you know it's a male?"

"I'm a journalist, it's my job to read people," Mpho replied as he gave his phone to the captain. "To listen not just to what they say but what they choose not to say."

"Premeditator@kubcity.kub," Sithole began. kubcity.kub was as official to the city as gov.za was to the country. Sithole groaned, knowing that to the point of the CSI, they were being mocked. "Subject, 'I Want To Trust You.'"

Dear Mr Journalist

"He doesn't refer to you by name."

"He has a tendency of not doing so, yes."

"Tendency? How many times have you spoken to him?"

Mpho swallowed nervously. "What do you mean?"

"How many times have you spoken to him?" Thabiso yelled, hitting the table with his fist.

"Once," he lied.

"Remember to check the call log once we're done," Sithole instructed the detective. He asked Mpho to unlock his phone again then he continued reading.

I do hope this finds you well.

You wrote an article recently about the unfortunate first incident. And I have to give credit to where it's due, it intrigued me. You seem like someone interested in all sides of the story rather than the single general opinion brainwashed into the public. For this reason, I believe it would be beneficial for us to talk.

"Here is a way to contact me," Sithole concluded. "This is a Cape Town number."

"He's smart," Simelane commented.

"Earlier, you mentioned that one of my officers, or rather, detectives went rogue and has done more than, how did you put it, 'the rest of your officers have combined.' What did you mean by that?"

Mpho's heart leapt to his throat. "It's just something I heard through the grapevine."

"Of course, you are a journalist after all. Thank you," the captain stood. "As soon as this email has been forwarded to me, you'll have your phone back and you'll be able to leave."

"What? No," Mpho argued as he rose from his seat. "He wants me to call. If someone else calls, who knows how he'll react? That is not something that can be risked."

"You said he already called you."

"And now he wants me to call him. He wants someone to tell his story, not someone who is ready to put him in handcuffs, amufake estokisini."

"We cannot let a civilian be dragged into this mess of a situation."

"Well, that's too bad because I seem to know more about this 'mess' than the two of you combined. With all due respect. Now, I didn't come here so that you can tell me to stay away for my own safety. I came here because I thought you might be able to use your brains and do that triangle thing from the movies where you track the call."

The captain and the detective looked at each other puzzled.

"Triangulation?" Thabiso corrected.

"Yes, that. Can you do it?"

"Watch him while I get a team in here," the captain instructed as he left the room.

CHAPTER 18

THE NTETHA & CO. BUILDING was quiet when Mandisa arrived. There were no more journalists, no police vehicles or personnel, no crowd of bystanders. This was probably going to be much easier than she expected she thought as she put on a pair of eyeglasses, and tied her hair. Stepping out of the car, she looked up at the towering building, at the top was the iconic Ntetha logo. As she walked through the sliding glass doors, a waft of lavender washed over her with a cool breeze. She knew she couldn't walk through the foyer without passing by the receptionist. There was no way around, forcing her to go through.

"Good morning and welcome to Ntetha Tower," said the receptionist. "Whom are you visiting today?"

"My lawyer," Mandisa replied.

"Will that be at Biyela & Co. or at Singh, Govender, Maharaj?"

"Biyela & Co."

The receptionist ran her fingers along the keyboard of her computer then looked up again. "Who will you be seeing ma'am, if you don't mind my asking?"

"Actually, I do."

"It's just protocol ma'am."

Mandisa glanced over her shoulder for a moment. "So is this," she pulled her badge out for a moment, allowing the receptionist enough time to identify it before she tucked it away.

"Apologies detective. It's the twenty-second floor," she indicated to the elevators.

"Thank you," Mandisa replied as relief washed over her. Without hesitation she made her way to the elevators, catching one just before the door closed. With a nod, she greeted those inside and pushed the button labelled 22. Through the mirrors of the elevator, the detective could see those behind her looking at her oddly. As their eyes met with hers, their heads shot down.

After a moment, the elevator stopped, and a man excused himself, hurrying out as the doors opened. The doors closed and the elevator continued its ascension, stopping again on the eighteenth floor, where the other two who were behind her stepped out, leaving her alone for the remaining four-floor rise.

She stepped out on the twenty-second floor, where she immediately saw another receptionist seated behind a dark wooden desk with a gold BIYELA & CO. written across it. She hurried to the desk and greeted the woman behind it.

"Welcome to—"

"I'm so sorry to cut you off, I have a meeting with Mr..." she closed her eyes and clicked her fingers in thought. "What's his name, agh, and I'm already late. May I please use your bathroom quickly?"

"Of course, it's just down the hall," she indicated to her left. "Second door on your right."

"Thank you so much," she rushed down the hall and into the women's bathroom.

Two women chatting away at the long marble sink turned to her. She moved to wash her hands at the farthest sink and dried them using the hot air hand drier. Looking at the mirror, she played with her hair a little before being happy with how it was set. Again, she washed her hands and dried them. She glanced over her shoulder before leaving the bathroom and continuing down the hallway in the opposite direction of the reception. As she walked, she glanced around the floor, separated by glass walls and doors. One corner office stood out to her; its glass was tinted with a misty grey colour to hide what was inside. The detective approached the office with caution, ensuring no one was watching her. Next to the door of the office was a digit passcode panel. Mandisa pulled out her taser and gave the panel a quick zap. In response, the door opened, and Mandisa quickly stepped inside, closing the door behind herself.

She covered her nose as death flooded her senses. There was no corpse, but the office had yet to be cleaned. The "YOU WERE WARNED!" message painted on the glass stood out to her as she looked around the room. Nozizwe was a woman, she had to have kept some perfume in the office, Mandisa thought as she slipped a pair of gloves on. She moved around the table and pulled open the first drawer, then the second, where she found a bottle of Expression by Bev. She uncapped the bottle, sprayed a dash on her wrist and brought it to her nose. She shook her head at the expensive smell. It seemed to wash out the bad smell of the room. Returning the bottle to its place, Mandisa closed the drawer.

The detective concluded that the office was in too much of a messy state to find any document in particular, even if she knew what she was looking for, which she did not. She turned to face the bold writing on the window.

"YOU WERE WARNED!"

Who was warned? Warned by who? Warned about what? Was it a final message to Nozizwe from the killer? Or was it a statement to someone else? A cop? Detective? The captain? Herself? Mandisa cut off the trailing questions. She didn't have the answers to them.

The detective got on her knees and searched below the wooden table. There was nothing to be found. Then she tried the remaining drawers, and again, to her disappointment, there was nothing of interest. Her eyes darted to the two-piece wooden cabinet with a glass tabletop – on which three glasses and a few bottles of strong liquor were set – then back to the table before her. She flipped a few documents on the table then tossed them aside deeply exhaling. Again, she glanced at the liquor table. She was less interested in the expensive alcohol, and more drawn by the wooden cabinets below them. She slowly walked over to the table and got on one knee. She opened the right cabinet, only to find more liquor. With a sigh, she closed it. As her heart thumped in her chest, she opened the left cabinet. Inside, a safe. Not exactly what she was hoping to come across, but it was as good a sign as she could get. She quickly took a picture of the safe and sent it to her safe cracker with the message "forgot my code." A few impatient moments later, her phone vibrated in her hand. She accepted the call and put her phone to her ear.

The voice spoke almost quietly, explaining what safe it was. *"So, the lock is electric based. Therefore, if you ever forget your code, it's pretty easy to open. You just need anything that has some alcohol in it, like actual alcohol, or hand sanitiser, and you'll also need a source of electricity."*

"Will a taser work?"

"It'll have to do, but be careful with it, as it may give you a bit of a jolt."

"What do I do?"

"Place the taser next to the lock, and as you pour the alcohol, hit the taser."

"This sounds dangerous."

"And it is, I don't recommend you go through with it."

"I don't have much of a choice," said Mandisa. "I need what's inside." After giving her gratitude, she ended the call. She pulled out her taser and slipped off her shoe, placing them both on the floor. She carefully lifted a liquor bottle from the glass table and screwed off the cap. Having everything she needed lined up in front of her, she slipped her left hand into her shoe, placed the taser onto the safe and held it in place with her shoe-protected hand. As she grabbed the bottle with her unoccupied hand, she realized her plan wouldn't work because she couldn't hit the taser's button. With a sigh, she replaced everything on the floor. Taking a big risk, she followed the correct instructions, pouring liquor as she tased the safe. Mandisa fell back as sparks flew from the safe.

"Dammit." The detective took a swing of the liquor in hand and closed her eyes as it burnt down her throat. When she lowered the bottle, she saw that the safe was open.

Inside the safe, was a piece of paper folded multiple times and held together by a paper click. Mandisa pulled it out and unfolded it.

12 Doctor Malibongwe Msimang Street, Ntabeni, KwaZulu Union Bay City.

CHAPTER 19

MEANWHILE, IN A DOUBLE-storey glass mansion in the uptown suburban area of Union Bay City, the doorbell rang. The owner casually dressed, sat in an oversized white furnished living room. His feet on the coffee table. Bottle of beer in hand, he sat watching a rugby game.

A woman dressed in a neat brown and blue uniform, trimmed with a traditional pattern stepped into the room. "Sir, someone is here to see you."

"I'm busy," the man replied, pointing his bottle to the television screen.

"Sir, I'm afraid he insists."

"So I should leave something important to attend to someone who may be irrelevant?" Turning to Rose, "That's not a rhetorical... question." Recognizing the man now standing behind Rose, he sighed.

Rose turned to see the guest now standing behind her. She stepped aside to make way for him.

"Thank you Rose."

Turning to the guest, Rose offered, "Sir, can I get you anything to drink?"

"Yes, some—"

"No," the house owner interrupted. "Thank you Rose."

"Yes sir," Rose sheepishly left the room.

"I'm sorry to—"

"Sit down."

"Look—"

"I said, sit down."

Swallowing awkwardly, the guest followed the instructions given. He shifted on the sofa a few times before settling as his host glared at him.

"You have the audacity to show up to my house, and let yourself in like you own the place, then apologize for doing exactly that."

"I'm sorry."

"Stop apologizing and tell me what you're doing in my house."

"What? You... you've seen the news, haven't you? This thing of the Premeditator? The kingpin is dead. The lawyer is dead. The organizer is dead."

"Zenzele died of natural cause last year."

"Regardless. That leaves the two of us."

"Let me tell you something," he sighed. "In this life, you're either one of two things. You're either the predator, or you are the prey. And I don't know about you, but I chose the former. So tell me something. Are you the predator or the prey?"

"How can you ask me that?"

"Are you scared?"

"What kind of question is that?"

"A nonrhetorical one. Are, you, scared?"

"Yes, of course, I'm scared."

"Then tell me something. Are you more afraid of dying, or having your reputation tarnished?"

"I never liked you," the guest exclaimed.

"It's taken you close to two decades to get that off your chest, it must feel real good."

"Maybe, but up until now I didn't realize that you're unhinged."

"That's a personal option therefore it does not affect me in any way."

"So what, you're just going to ignore this?"

"Like I said, predator and prey."

"You're a piece of trash, you know that."

Pulling a gun out of the gap of his couch, he aimed at his guest, "You want to say that again? Come on, I dare you."

The guest shrunk in his seat.

"I don't know where you find the audacity to come into my house and call me unhinged," he waved the gun around. "Yeah, I may be a piece of trash but at least I'm a smart piece of trash you dimwit."

"Given the circumstances, I suppose there's no reason for us to remain in contact."

"You bet your coward behind that this is where our association ends. I've worked too hard to get to where I am to just be disrespected, in my own house no less, by the likes of you. I don't know what Zenzele saw in you. Now please get out of my house before I have to call security."

"You will die sad and alone."

"And you will die a man who forsook his values and beliefs. Now get. Out. Of my house."

CHAPTER 20

IT DIDN'T TAKE MUCH time to get the tech team to set everything up for the call to the Premeditator. Trying to keep the situation hushed at the station proved to be difficult. The rushing around of the officers that Sithole specifically chose for the operation of the call caused a lot of whispers and drew a lot of eyes. The captain had instructed Mpho to keep the conversation going for at least a minute, two if he could. They needed pinpoint accuracy, so they don't make the mistake of finding themselves pouring every resource at their disposal going to the wrong location. They couldn't afford to make any mistake. Not with a chance like this, when the stakes were so high. The door was closed, locking Mpho, Sithole, Thabiso, Jabu, and two members of the tech team inside.

"We're ready," one of the techies said.

"Okay, make the call," the captain instructed.

The techy nodded and hit the call button on the station's phone. It rang for what felt like hours before it was answered. Nothing but slow shallow breaths came through.

"Hello?" Mpho began.

"*Hello journalist,*" the deep computer-modified voice came through.

Mpho's heart began to beat against his ribs as if trying to escape his body.

"*It took you a while.*"

Mpho lifted his eyes to the captain.

"Relax, relax," Sithole mouthed.

He took a deep breath and released it. Fixing his eyes on the phone once more, he said, "Well, it's not often I receive an email from an interesting character such as yourself."

"*I thank you for your reservation of insults. It is much appreciated.*"

"You wanted to talk, here I am."

"*Considering your profession, I thought you'd be more hospitable. However, I cannot blame you, you probably suffer from as much a lack of information as the rest of this city.*"

"You want to share that information with me? You want your story to be told?"

Concerned by the silence, Mpho looked up to the captain, who lifted both hands and started folding a finger by the second.

"You want me to tell your story?"

"*That's subjective.*"

"How do you mean?"

"*I don't want you to tell my story. I want people to understand the whole story. It's not just about seeing but perceiving. People celebrate politicians, the rich and famous. But as soon as you unveil the true colours of these praised people, the general public seizes to believe in them.*"

"You're trying to prove that these high-status people are still at the end of the day, human."

"*I'm not trying, I'm succeeding, there is a difference. However, many people are not fans of others succeeding, even when it is beneficial to themselves. People such as the police.*"

Mpho looked up at the officers surrounding him. "People don't want to see others winning," he mumbled.

"*You can stop stalling now.*"

"Stalling?"

"*If the police you're with haven't found my location by now, you should be very concerned.*"

"What makes you think I'm with the police."

"*You have twenty minutes before I destroy everything and switch locations*," as always, the line went dead.

"Exactly two minutes. Did you get it?" the captain shouted.

"Yes sir," a man replied from behind his computer screen.

"Then let's move."

He's toying with us, the journalist thought to himself as the officers moved around him, rushing to leave. *He's one step ahead at every moment. How do you win a game you can't play? No. How do you beat the creator of the game?*

"Mpho!" a voice snapped the journalist from his thoughts. "Let's go, he'll want to see you, talk to you."

With the captain, Mpho left the station as they began their drive to the presumed location of the Premeditator.

"Wire him up."

"Yes sir," an officer sitting in the back seat with Mpho complied.

"Is this necessary?"

"Yes," Sithole replied. "Like I said, he'll want to talk to you. We can't go in until he admits with his own mouth, that he killed Mkhonto and Nozizwe. Even if he admits to only one of the two, that's our green light to storm in. Can you drive?"

"Yes."

"Good." From the passenger's seat, the captain held up a tablet indicating the route. "You'll take Thabiso's car and we'll be parked down the road. You have to make him say he killed them, got it?"

"Yeah."

"And please don't touch the mic, don't scratch your chest and don't try to talk into it. We'll be able to hear you perfectly fine. If he suspects that you're wired, we're done."

"I understand."

The cars pulled to a stop.

"Let's go," the captain stepped out of the vehicle.

Thabiso was already walking over with his car keys in hand. "Mission's a go?"

"Yes," the captain replied.

"Don't mess up my car," the detective placed his keys in Mpho's hand. "Or we'll have a problem," he whispered.

CHAPTER 21

IN THE OFFICE OF VIHAAN Naicker, at Union Bay City Bank, the CEO stood at the window, staring down at the city below him. A now cold cup of coffee still in hand. He couldn't help but ponder on how disappointed the Founding Five from twelve years ago would be if they saw what had become of their beloved city in a matter of a day. He may not have liked the Kingpin, but he knew that he was a necessary evil. The only line keeping crime in check. And now, he was no more. The criminal kingdom had lost its king, and dozens were fighting to take his place. There had been at least four reported shootings and eleven confirmed deaths in a single day. That had been unprecedented for Union Bay. The only gang war worse than this was that which took place in 2012, which claimed the lives of many gang men and more civilians in an all-out war. Still caught deep in thought, he didn't hear the repeated knock on his door before his secretary let herself in.

"Sir?" she disturbed, yelling loud enough for the whole office floor to hear.

Vihaan turned and immediately noticed the envelope in her hands. His eyes were heavy and slowly reddening. "Is that for me?" he asked, his voice much less enthusiastic than usual.

"Yes, sir, it is."

With a low sigh, he turned away from the window. For a moment, he tried to ignore the horrors on the other side of the glass. "Who is it from?"

The secretary turned the envelope in her hands to show Vihaan both of its sides. "It doesn't say. It's just blank."

"Thank you. You could umm..." he closed his eyes, then struggled to reopen them. "You can just leave it on the table," he instructed, before yawning.

Complying, the secretary left the note on the table and offered to take his cup.

Looking down at his coffee, the CEO replied, "It's okay, thanks."

As the glass door closed, Vihaan walked over to his table and sighed as he pulled out a paper bag-wrapped glass bottle and emptied its little remaining contents into the cup. After gulping down his liquid concoction, the CEO picked up the envelope and ran his thumb along the front of the fine material. On the bottom right corner, he felt something embossed, his brow furrowed. He couldn't make out what it was, but he guessed it to be a symbol. Every bit of anonymous mail he had ever received always made him nervous, and this was no different. Shaking the feeling, he opened the envelope and emptied its contents onto the table, a letter, a USB and a syringe filled with a clear-looking substance he did not recognize. The space between his eyebrows almost disappeared as his eyes ran down the letter. Putting the letter aside, the CEO rushed around his table and shoved the USB into his laptop. Within seconds, new windows started opening across the screen throwing him back on his chair and making his breathing heavier. Document after document filled the screen and terror filled his eyes.

CHAPTER 22

THE DRIVE TO THE ADDRESS was short. Mandisa was in no rush, and it took her under an hour. She could feel chills flowing down her spine as she realised where her GPS had pinned her destination. A not-so-old theme park that was shut down mere months after Ntetha & Co. opened their own high-end multimillion-Rand theme park and museum about 5 kilometres outside the City Centre in 2009. Which was just in time for the FIFA World Cup that was hosted in South Africa the following year. Mandisa had heard about this theme park growing up, but she never had the chance to visit because her parents were always working, or didn't have the money, automatically giving the Premeditator the home-ground advantage. The detective glanced at the time on her radio before stepping out of her car, onto the empty parking lot.

16:43.

She pulled her unregistered firearm from its holster, released the magazine, did a quick count of the bullets then clicked it back in place. Nine bullets should be enough, she thought. Are they? she considered as she looked at the deserted park. She reached into the compartment between the chairs of her car and pulled out a full magazine. Almost satisfied, she tucked it into her back pocket. None of the pockets of her jeans were as loose as she would've preferred for the purpose she wanted them to serve at the moment. However, the back pocket felt more convenient than either of the front pockets. She reached over the driver's seat again, pulled another magazine out and slipped it in next to the first, making the hug of her denim tighter on her curves. Feeling a little more confident, the detective closed the storage compartment, closed her door, locked the car, and pulled on the handle to check that it was locked. Mandisa replaced her gun in the holster as she walked towards the main park premises.

The large gates decorated with the park's name swung open as she approached. That was a sign that she was at the right place if she still had any scepticism. Mandisa felt her spirit almost jump out of her body as the speakers crackled.

"Welcome to Day at the Bay theme park," a tender voice came through the harsh old speakers.

The pre-recorded message they played every morning, the detective thought to herself.

"We're so glad to have you today."

Mandisa waited for the voice to continue. Instead, it was replaced by a deeper, firmer and less enthusiastic voice. "Hello detective," no computer modulation.

Mandisa immediately recognised the voice from the call she received at Mthandazo's office earlier in the day.

"Don't bother trying to speak, I can't hear you from where I am. I wonder, how's the riddle going? Have you figured it out?" For a moment, the speakers hummed. "You may not be able to see me, but I assure you that I see you. A nod will suffice if you have figured out the riddle."

Mandisa decided not to play along.

"I assume you want to find me, see the face behind the voice, the man who brought Union Bay to its knees. So, how about we play a game? A riddle to start. A single life is like a bomb, and the end is at the heart. You have ten minutes to figure me out, when the clock hits five, you'll be too late. That's the riddle, man's dilemma, no time to diddle, what am I?"

Mandisa took a moment to consider the riddle together with her surroundings. Life, bomb, end, heart. Amusement Park. "A maze," the detective whispered. She rushed to the closest map of the park, found the maze's location then traced it back to the YOU ARE HERE. She checked her watch.

16:49.

When the clock hits five, she considered. Five o'clock. The detective pulled out her phone and set the Timer to nine minutes thirty seconds as she rushed to the maze.

"I think it's time for a serious conversation. When you said that we are 'not a team.' That hurt my feelings a little. But I forgive you. I thought you would understand what it's like for no one to believe you, for everyone to turn their back on you, just like your colleagues did to you."

Mandisa was left with just under nine minutes on her Timer when she entered the overgrown hedges. On the first turn, she had to take was plastered a maze poster and a pen was stabbed at the bottom of it. Above the maze was a table of the alphabet and the numbers 1 – 26 in the row below. Under the table were the words.

Solve the questions below to complete the sentence.

$27 - 14 = \underline{}$

$25 \div 5 = \underline{}$

$6 + 7 = \underline{}$

$4 \times 4 - 1 = \underline{}$

$3(2 + 7) - 9 = \underline{}$

$\underline{} \times 10 - 70 = 180$

To complete the maze, you will need to use your _____. The use of your **phone** or **calculator** is **prohibited** and has **lethal consequences**.

"Which reminds me," the voice persisted.

The detective groaned wishing the speakers would go quiet.

"I forgot to tell you that if you decide to irresponsibly call the police, not that you're not an officer yourself, anyway, my point is, if you call anyone, especially the station, let's just say things won't end well."

Mandisa grabbed the pen and answered the first three questions which were simple, 13, 5, and 13. From the fourth question, she had to exercise her brain muscles a little more.

$4 \times 4 - 1 = \underline{}$

She took a moment to think then she wrote 15. The last two questions frustrated her just looking at them.

$3(2 + 7) - 9 = \underline{}$

$\underline{} \times 10 - 70 = 180$

She thought about checking her Timer, then glanced at the rule again.

The use of your **phone** or **calculator** is **prohibited** and has **lethal consequences**.

She cursed beneath her breath before scrabbling her mind for the answer. On her palm, she wrote:

$6 + 21$

$= 27 - 9$

$= 18.$

She wrote 18 on the poster. Mandisa knew guessing her way to the answer of the last question would take too long so she decided to work it backwards. She rolled up her left sleeve and wrote the equation:

$180 + 70 \div 10 = X.$

$180 + 7 = 187.$

That couldn't be the answer, so she drew a line through it and reconsidered. Lower on her forearm she wrote:

$250 \div 10.$ Then draw a line over the zeros:

$2\cancel{5}\cancel{0} \div 1\cancel{0}.$

Satisfied, she wrote 25 on the poster then looked at the table of alphabets and numbers. Using the table as a reference, she wrote the missing word, **MEMORY**.

To complete the maze, you will need to use your **MEMORY**.

Mandisa quickly drew her way through the maze from the YOU ARE HERE to the centre.

"Right, left, right, left, left, right, right, left, left, right, left, left, right, left, left, left," she memorised. Once she was happy that she knew the way, she pulled out her gun, checked the magazine again, clicked it back in place, pulled back the slide then released it. Taking the first right turn, the detective held her gun close, trying to walk as quickly as she could and checking each new turn before taking it. The deeper into the maze she got, the narrower the halls became and the turns she had to take drew closer to each other in distance. Two turns away, she felt a wire tug on her ankle. Instinctively she ducked and pulled her trigger twice aiming forward. She waited a moment, but nothing happened. As she rose from her position, the speakers crackled again.

"I think I finally understand why you say we're not a team. You think yourself higher than me. But in truth, you are not."

Mandisa cautiously continued.

"What you have to understand is that you, detective, are one mere bad day away from being me."

"I've had bad days, but I'll never be you."

"You're almost there."

The detective turned around the last corner.

"Congratulations, you've found me."

Mandisa exhaled, her eyes red, skin boiling as she looked at the monitors spread across a table in the centre of the end of the maze. The monitors all showed a different location.

"But so have they. Goodbye, detective," the speakers died off.

The main monitor flickered to a camera feed from a ceiling view showing two men seated across from each other in a lowly lit apartment dining room.

Mandisa took a step closer to the monitors, trying to observe clearly as one of the two men's voices spoke through the speakers of the room.

"*...they don't play with the same rules that we play with! They think they're above us,*" one of the voices concluded.

"*You don't get to decide what happens to people.*"

Mandisa narrowed her eyes at the recognition of the voice. She focused on the clothes of the man she thought she knew then she realized who it was.

"*But they do?*" the other voice questioned.

Mandisa watched as lights flooded the room, men in black marching in with their guns raised.

CHAPTER 23

MPHO COULD FEEL THE bullets of sweat trickling down his face as he drove down the road to an old-looking apartment building he had never seen or heard of before. This was, after all, the least talked about place in Union Bay. Every city had its dangerous places, and this was that place for KUB City. He could still feel his heart thumping against his chest as he walked up the stairs of the building. As he walked past every open door, he peeked in, and tested the closed doors, they all opened but darkness filled all the rooms. On the third floor, Mpho could see a bit of light slipping beneath a closed door. He prepared himself and grabbed the handle. As he opened the door, the light went off. It was a candle next to the door and the breeze was just strong enough to snuff it out. Darkness enveloped the journalist as he walked in.

"Cartel Kingpin Killed Following Premeditator's Appearance," a voice called out. "That's quite the title, Mpho Seme."

Mpho's breathing quickened.

"There's a clock behind you, tell me. What time is it?"

Cautiously, the journalist turned his head to glance at the clock then just as quickly turned back to the man he was yet to make out in the shadows. Again, he glanced back then turned his attention back to the shadows before him, "It's almost five."

"What's the matter, you can't read time?"

"I can."

"Then tell me, what time is it?"

Confused and curious, Mpho glanced at the clock again. "It's four, forty-nine."

"Thank you. Now please, take a seat."

Mpho pulled a chair back from the table and ran his hand over it quickly before sitting.

"Do you not trust me?"

"Are you—"

"Shh," the voice interrupted.

The tick of the clock filled the room as Mpho remained silent, waiting for his host to speak.

"I wonder, where did the detective run off to."

The journalist opened his mouth to answer but no response came.

"You were with her, were you not?"

Mpho got nervous that the police listening in might have heard that. "For a moment. But she's not exactly the nicest person to encounter. And she's not someone who shares information or asks for permission."

"Interesting observation. However, the more relevant question is why are you here?"

Raising his voice, "You wanted me here," Mpho replied.

"So, what, you came running?"

"What do you want from me?"

"You came to me, should I not be asking you that question?"

The voice of the captain in Mpho's head forced him to calm down. "I want to help you," he sighed.

"What makes you think I need your help?"

"You could say it's just a hunch."

"A journalist's instincts?"

"I suppose."

"You had me curious, but now you have me intrigued. How exactly can *you* help me?"

"I can tell the story you want everyone to understand. Coming from you it seems biased, but coming from someone else—"

"Coming from you," the voice interjected.

"Coming from me, maybe people might give it a little more attention."

"You can make them understand?"

"I can try my best," Mpho assured. "Right now, you have a lot of people worried, concerned, fearful. You let me tell the story and people might not fear you. Instead, they might just sympathize," the journalist explained. "People love stories, that's why Union Bay City News is still so popular. Stories are embedded in our DNA."

"You thought this was about the Founding Five. You were wrong, partially. It's about the corruption of the city which goes deep into the roots of its very foundation. The people who are trusted are those most toxic to our communities."

"Then why kill? Why not let them be arrested?"

"The man you called the kingpin, called Mkhonto... was known for his many crimes, yet he continued to roam our streets like any other man."

"The police were still investigating him."

"If you cut a tree down, it will grow again. But if you uproot it completely, it is dead forever," the voice replied as his figure stepped out of the shadows.

Mpho's heart jumped to his throat making it nearly impossible to swallow.

"You— many people share your sentiment, but you're the only one standing up and doing something. I don't think you're a bad person," Mpho lied. "Just misunderstood. I don't think you wanted to kill Mkhonto or Nozizwe."

"But they deserved it. In fact, they had it easy. They made thousands of people suffer over the years, so I'd say they deserved so much worse than what they got. It's like you said, many people share my sentiment, they're just not willing to do what's necessary, to cross the threshold, to kill people like Mkhonto and Nozizwe."

"Because it's wrong," the journalist argued.

"So what? Right and wrong is a very thin line because they don't play with the same rules that we play with! They think they're above us."

"You don't get to decide what happens to people."

"But they do?"

Before any answer could formulate in Mpho's mind, the door was knocked in, figures dressed in full black flooded the room guns with flashlights washing the darkness out as they trailed on the man seated across from the journalist. Getting pushed aside, Mpho could only watch as the man he was just talking to got shoved onto the table, and tightly cuffed around his wrists. Getting lifted from his seat by the squad of men, Mandla glanced up at the camera on the ceiling. A smirk spread across his face before he was dragged out.

THE DETECTIVE'S STOMACH turned as the whitewashing lights faded from the screen. Mpho, who had been watching Mandla get dragged out walked around the table to the seat Mandla had occupied. He looked up, eyes narrowed, unknowingly creating eye contact with the detective.

Mandisa pulled out her phone and scrolled through her contact list to **Captain**. She hesitated, then she hit the call button. A bruising brick force struck the back of the detective's head before she could place the phone to her ear, dropping her with a massive thud. Wincing, she grabbed the back of her head, her vision fishing in and out of focus. She rolled onto her stomach. Shattering glass rang in her ears as she reached her right hand down to her waist, her fingers enveloping the metallic weapon. She narrowed her eyes at the source of the sound. As she was regaining focus, the figure hovered over her. She pulled out her gun, but a burning sensation reached her first, stinging her left eye and just missing her right as it burnt the skin of the upper section of her face.

Mandisa shut her right eye tight and stuck her face to the ground to prevent her right eye from getting exposed to the stinging spray. A final shatter of glass echoed before Mandisa heard a frantic voice.

Shaking, "I'm," the assailant choked. "I'm sorry."

Forcing herself to silence her pain, she focused her ear on the sound of footsteps as boot met grass. She took a silent breath. As she released it, she forced her body onto her left arm as she aimed at the leaving figure. Using her right eye to see the blurred figure, she pulled twice on her trigger.

Falling to his knees, the assailant scurried around the corner, cursing lowly as he disappeared.

The detective released three more shots into the hedges, hoping the bullets would brush through the thick hedges and meet her assailant. She sighed as she rolled onto her back, wincing a little as her head made contact with the ground below it. It was only then that she heard a voice coming from her phone.

"*Khuluma Xaba, ukuphi?*"

Mandisa grabbed her phone with her free hand and pressed the power button, ending the call. Forcing herself up, the detective saw the wreckage left from what was the monitors she had found. Discouraged, she returned her gun to its place and tried to remember the way out of the maze.

CHAPTER 24

SIRENS BLARED; LIGHTS painted the night blue as the police vehicles screeched to a stop outside the station. Almost in unison, the officers jumped out of their vehicles and surrounded the van, lifting their guns as Thabiso unlocked its door and swung it open. Mandla emerged from the darkness, flanked by two thin-lipped, narrow-eyed officers with their guns trailing him.

A blonde-haired officer approached Thabiso, his hand tightly squeezing the handle of his gun.

"James," the detective greeted. "Are the civilians all gone?"

"All cleared."

"Good." He looked at Mandla before turning back to the blonde. "Let's get this scum inside before someone sees him and starts asking questions." Motioning the officers to follow him, he led the way into the station, down the thin hallway, and into a tiny interrogation room that looked like it was last maintained decades ago.

Four officers positioned themselves in the corners of the room while two others chained Mandla to the table. Thabiso watched Mandla through the process. Mandla's lack of emotion infuriated the detective.

"Secured," said one of the officers who was chaining Mandla. He stepped out of the room, and his colleague followed him out. The heavy metal door was shut behind them.

"Mandla Magwaza, I'm Detective Simelane, but you will address me as Detective. I will ask you a series of questions and I expect you to answer, is that understood?"

Mandla shifted his weight on the seat to slouch ever so slightly.

"You are in a lot of trouble," the detective began. "Two murders in two days. You know where your problem started? You have an ego. You wanted to be seen. To be recognised as the man who brought havoc to the city. But what has that amounted to? Nothing. Look at where you are. Why did you kill Nozizwe Biyela?"

Mandla laced his fingers in response.

"Are you sure you want to stay quiet? Well, it's your fifty years you'd spend in prison," he shrugged. "Not mine." Thabiso knocked on the door. "I'll give you some time to think it over."

The door shrieked against the floor. Thabiso stepped out and closed it.

"You think he'll talk?" James fell into step with Thabiso.

"People tend to think a little clearly when they realise what's at stake. And in his case, he'll be losing what may just be the rest of his life. After two minutes, he'll be singing."

"Show him the carrot, not the stick."

"Exactly." Thabiso knocked on the door labelled **CAPTAIN**.

"He's not here," James revealed.

"You can't be serious. We need him here, where'd he go?"

"He didn't say, but I guess you're in charge for the time being."

Thabiso sighed and then checked his watch. "Mandisa still hasn't shown up?"

"Not yet."

"She's really making things more difficult than they have to be."

"What do you mean?"

"If she's not guilty, why is she not here? Because if Mandla really did kill Nozizwe and Mkhonto, that means she's innocent."

"Maybe she's trying to prove that she's innocent?"

"Then she shouldn't be running."

"Do you really think Mandla might not be the killer? That Mandisa might be capable of..."

"I know Mandla is not innocent. As for Xaba, it wouldn't be the first time she's gone too far."

"What do you mean?"

"Don't worry about it," he checked his watch again. "Let's see if Mandla wants to talk now." Thabiso left James pondering on their conversation as he returned to the interrogation room, stepped inside and took a seat across from Mandla. "You feeling in the spirit of talking yet?"

Mandla opened his mouth for a moment, then closed it again with a sigh.

"Hard to get doesn't work on me, you either want to talk or not. So, what will it be?"

Again, Mandla opened his mouth, this time just yarning.

"Now that's just rude." Thabiso got up from his chair. "If you still don't feel like talking, you can suit yourself." He walked to the door and banged on it twice.

The metal shrieked on the floor. Thabiso gave a final glance over his shoulder before walking out and shutting the door.

"Anything?" asked one of the officers guarding the door.

"No, uSithole usebuyile?"

"Yeah, in his office."

"Sho." Thabiso made his way to the captain's office. He gave a light tap on the wood. There was no response. He tried again with a slightly heavier hand."

"Ngena," the captain's voice called from the other side of the thick wood.

Thabiso let himself in, "Kapteni."

"Close the door," he continued his paperwork without lifting his head.

The detective gently closed the door and took a seat across the table from Sithole. "I just spoke to Mandla."

"Utheni?"

Thabiso hesitated, "akashongo lutho. He didn't respond to me, didn't argue, didn't defend himself. He just sat there, not saying a single thing."

"So, what does that mean for us?"

"Well, it could mean he's not innocent, but it doesn't exactly prove he's guilty."

Sithole's pen stopped moving across the page beneath it for the first time since Thabiso entered the office. Then he finally lifted his head. "It doesn't prove he's not guilty. He admitted to killing both Nozizwe and Mkhonto when he was talking to Mpho. What more do you want?"

"Something just doesn't feel right, sir."

"He slipped up, that's what we wanted. He's probably considering how he could get out of this situation, which he can't. What more do you expect from him?"

"To be honest, I'm not sure."

"Leave him be, it'll give him time to let the situation sink in completely." Sithole returned his focus to his paperwork. "The mayor wants this resolved as quickly and quietly as possible. It likely won't be quiet, but quick, maybe. And hopefully, it'll get the minister off my back."

"How so?"

"A judge agreed to try the case tomorrow morning."

"Then I guess we should be getting some rest. I'll have a look at social media, and see if the news has broken yet. Hopefully, it hasn't but just to be safe, I think it's best if we prepare to have everyone on the ready for a chaotic scene at the courthouse."

"Yeah," again Sithole stopped writing. "I'll call the other stations before I leave, let them know to prepare for the worst. And Xaba?"

"Two teams posted outside her place, but she hasn't been there."

Sithole nodded. "See you tomorrow."

"Yes sir," the detective got up from his seat walked to the door, turned the handle then looked over his shoulder. "Kapteni, if you don't mind my asking. Where were you?"

"I do mind."

Thabiso nodded and stepped out. The thought passed his mind to tell Mandla about tomorrow, to watch him react to knowing he's lost. He shook it off. It would be better to inform him in the morning to keep the element of surprise for as long as they could. Thabiso was finally starting to realize, Mandla only had as much power as the information he had could give him. Without control of information, he was powerless. This thought gave Thabiso some semblance of satisfaction as he stepped into his car and drove home.

CHAPTER 25

THE CLOCK WAS ABOUT to hit six when Mandisa walked up to the front door of a beautiful, unfenced house in a high-class private security-protected part of the city. A light-skinned woman was waiting to welcome her. "Top deck," Mandisa called out.

"Coconut," the woman replied.

"It's been too long."

"Well, that's what happens when you grow up."

"It's nice to know that you're still as literal as you've ever been Phume."

Mandisa closed the door as she looked around. Phume led her through the sleek and stylishly furnished house.

"So, this is how CA's live?"

"Well, not all," she reluctantly admitted. "A lot of people lost not just their jobs but their careers back in 19, 20, and 21. Not that they didn't try to get back on the horse, the horses just ran away. Make yourself at home," she took a seat on the single couch. The detective sat across from her. "I was one of the lucky ones who survived."

"You're not lucky, you're just good at what you do."

"And sprinkle a couple of blessings from Heaven in there, yes. I forgot you don't believe in luck. What is it you used to say about choices?"

"Everything has a choice; every choice has a consequence that—"

"Leads to another choice," Phume finished off with a smile. "Anyway."

Mandisa's phone rang. "Sorry," pulling out her phone, she checked the number, unsaved. She declined the call. "You were saying?"

"I had a look at the documents you sent me, then I had to double-check them, and then checked them again to be sure since I couldn't send it for a second opinion given it came from... well you."

"You really didn't have to make such a big deal about it Phume."

"In accounting, efficiency is everything," Phume argued.

Mandisa's phone pinged.

"And from the look of things, there's nothing illegal here."

The detective checked the message on her phone.

It's Thando. The safe is open.

"Mandisa?"

"Hmm? Sorry, I just need to take this, it's a bit of an emergency."

"It's okay," Phume got up. "You can take your time," she left the room.

Mandisa opened her recent call logs and called the number at the top. After two rings, it was answered.

"*Detective. You won't believe what we found.*"

"Who is we?"

"*Well, me and Mpumelelo. Your guy left as soon as the safe was unlocked, he didn't even open it. But I guess that's the point of a safe, to keep all of your secrets safe. He was really professional and—*"

"Thando."

"*Yeah?*"

"The safe."

"*Oh right. Okay, so there was a bunch of documents, but most of them are redacted so I'm not sure how much of help they will be to you.*"

"I'll come by tonight to pick them up."

"*Okay, but depending on what time it is you might not catch me; I'll be at church from six. But Bheka will be home, so I'll let him know to expect you.*"

"Okay, thanks. And Thando."

"*Yeah?*"

"Whatever you found in that safe stays between you, me your brother."

"*Well, Mpumelelo will likely tell uMa, but I can try to talk him out of it. I don't know if she asked him.*"

"Then it stays between the four of us."

"*Okay, choi.*" The line went dead.

"Phume?"

"Ngiyeza," the accountant responded from another room. "I got you a little something." She walked into the room carrying two cups of cold beverages in glass cups. "Ice cappuccino."

"You too good for regular coffee?"

"Hey, it's your fault I drink this." She handed Mandisa a cup and took a sip from her own. "You used to love it when we were still in uni. It's not my fault you became a cop and now live off coffee and doughnuts."

"I can't believe you just used that stereotype." She took a sip of the cappuccino. Satisfaction washed over her.

"Okay, so as I was saying. What was I saying?"

They both took a moment to think. "Nothing illegal," Mandisa remembered.

"Oh, right, okay so people misunderstand embezzlement, and of course, that's with good reason. So, all it is," she spoke between sips, "is the intentional misappropriation of assets entrusted upon a certain individual by an organization with the expectation that said individual can and will protect said assets for, and only for," she emphasized, "their intended use."

"Okay. So can you now say all of that in simplified English please."

"This money wasn't embezzled," the accountant explained. "It was just... shifted around to make it seem that way."

Mandisa looked over her cup thoughtfully as she drank her cappuccino. "So, it was strategically sent from the company's account to the mysterious individual's account, then later reversed?"

"That's the highly oversimplified version of it but yes. However, they took it one step further by sending it through the bank before sending it to the individual's account. They probably did that thinking it was a way of cleaning the money, but it was a bit unnecessary. But then again, sending it through the bank reduces questions thereby taking any sniffing noses, like cops, no offence, off their trail."

"None taken."

"Yeah, so nothing illegal was done. But with that being said, don't get me wrong, I love you and all, but if this has to do with any shady or dangerous business..."

"You want nothing to do with it, I know," Mandisa interjected. "You have nothing to worry about. I was never here, and you never saw these documents."

She handed the file to Mandisa. "You know, that never seems to reassure me cause you worry me every time you say it."

"I owe you one."

"Technically you owe me a lot. But remember, I'll hold you to that."

"Don't tell me you're recording this."

"I'm an accountant, I record every transaction, friendly or business. I'm joking. But seriously, I'll hold you to it."

After thanking the accountant and finishing her cold beverage, Mandisa showed herself out.

CHAPTER 26

KWAZULU UNION BAY GENERAL Hospital, better known as Union Bay General or KUB Gen, was unusually quiet tonight. The detective guessed it was a result of it being so late. She realized she was wrong when she saw the visiting hours board. She was just over an hour too late. However, she walked through the entrance with determination. She greeted the receptionist enthusiastically.

"Welcome to Union Bay General, how may I assist you ma'am?" the lady replied from the other side of the desk.

"I'm here to see Mr Bayanda Zondi."

"Oh," the receptionist frowned. "Unfortunately visiting hours are over."

"I think you should be able to make an exception given that he's the victim of an ongoing investigation," she pulled her badge out to exhibit to the receptionist.

The lady glanced at Mandisa's badge then looked back up. "I... please give me a moment." She disappeared into an adjacent room. After a few moments, she stepped out with an older woman, who assessed the detective with narrow eyes while listening to the receptionist.

The older woman whispered something to the receptionist then approached the table, "It's quite late, detective...?"

"Xaba. I understand, however, I have a few questions that can't wait," she lied. "It will only take a moment."

The older woman sighed. "Follow me." She moved around the table and led Mandisa to the elevators. They took one to the seventh floor. Mandisa still remembered the way to the room, but she followed from a safe distance behind. They stopped at the entrance of a ward, where a nurse was busy with a pile of papers. "Nurse."

"Yebo."

"This is Detective Xaba, she's here to see a patient of yours."

"Bayanda Zondi," Mandisa added. "He was the victim of an assault connected to a..." she juggled her word choice, "sensitive case. I have reason to believe that he could be highly instrumental to the outcome of the investigation."

"I'm sorry to hear that."

"Is it possible to speak to him?"

"I'm afraid not. You're a few minutes too late."

"Uselele?"

"No. He was moved this afternoon."

"To another ward?"

"Another hospital, I wasn't given the details."

"Do you know who was?"

"Doctor Chetty. But that's why I said you're a few minutes too late, he left at eight o'clock, and he'll only be back on Monday."

Mandisa checked her watch and sighed. **20:08.**

"I wish I could help you, but I really can't. But I do hope you find him."

Mandisa nodded.

"I'll walk you out."

"It's okay, I remember the way." After thanking the women for their time, Mandisa showed herself out and back to her car.

CHAPTER 27

THE CLOCK HAD JUST struck nine when Mandisa arrived at the Msani mansion. She drove much slower than usual, distracted by the thought of Bayanda's sudden hospital move. Finding him was going to be difficult, given her lack of connections to hospital staff. But she knew difficult did not mean impossible.

Her knock on the door was quickly answered. This time by the butler, Mr Bhekumuzi Gwala. "Detective Xaba," he greeted. "Miss Msani will be with you shortly." He stepped aside to allow the detective in. Mandisa knew quite a bit about Gwala because of the investigation into Zenzele's death the previous year. He had been working for the Msani family for close to thirty years and he became a close and trusted friend of Zenzele. He had an interesting demeanour. But what intrigued Mandisa most about the well-aged man was why a former military man would become a butler. A question to which she accepted she may never get the answer. "May I get you anything? I could have the chefs whip something up for you before they return to their quarters."

"It's okay, I don't think I will stay long."

"Rubbish," Thando yelled from the top of the curving staircase. "She never wants to have anything. It's weird because other guests try to finish our entire fridge, and want to taste half our wine collection." She walked down the stairs to meet Mandisa in the lobby. "Please dish up a bit of the supper for us, we'll be in the dining in a minute."

With a nod, the butler disappeared into the next room.

"Thando..."

"Ah, ah, don't 'Thando' me. You're a detective outside, but in this house, you're a guest. And uMa told me her conditions. So, either we eat while we work, or I have the food packed for you to go home with but without the documents because there's no way you had time to go home and cook. In fact, I'm not convinced you've eaten or had some rest since the last time I saw you."

Mandisa sighed audibly.

"Exactly. The file is in the office." Thando led the detective back to the home office, where a file folder was waiting in the slightly opened safe. "But like I said on the phone, I'm not sure you'll get much from this." She handed the folder to Mandisa. "Now come on, let's get some food in you."

By the time they got to the dining room, Bheka had set up the two plates with cutlery and a few dishing mini pots on the white-clothed table. The detective looked at Thando, suppressing a sigh.

"Don't look at me, you heard me say 'a bit,' you were there". Thando removed the lids of the pots. "You spread out the papers and I'll dish up."

Exhaling heavily, Mandisa opened the folder and started placing the papers out on the other end of the table. Every document she laid out was as Thando mentioned; redacted. Some had more black patches than they had white. The similarity they all shared was having dates. That's how Mandisa tried to sort them on the table, from the earliest date to the most recent. Once they were all on the table, there were only about fourteen documents, each with pages ranging from two to seven. If she were to guess, she'd say there's an estimate of fifty to seventy pages to go through.

"Not that many," said Thando as she approached the detective.

"That's not necessarily a good thing."

"Yeah, but I mean most of it is redacted anyway so it'll make it easy to go through."

"We technically don't know what we're looking for, so that makes it a needle in a haystack," as Mandisa stepped back, she noticed that Thando was done dishing up for them. "Suppose it's better to start by eating."

"You don't have to tell me twice."

While eating, they chatted about how life had been since they met towards the end of last year. Thando commented on how devasted the family would've been that her father could've been killed if the chronic disease, which she didn't mention by name, hadn't taken him first. She almost cried speaking about how he kept the sickness a secret from the family – except his wife. The detective could only just listen, not knowing how she was to respond, her perception of her own father not as kind. They never spoke for the rest of the meal.

"I'll take these to the kitchen," Thando offered as she reached for Mandisa's plate.

The detective sighed as she watched her host walk away. She knew loss just as much as Thando did, yet she still never knew how to handle such a situation. The memory of the last day she spent with her mother tugged at her again. She shook it off and went over to the chronologically laid out documents. She took the first of the bunch. When Thando got back, she asked her to start from the most recent and work backwards while she started at the furthest date and worked forward. They would meet halfway.

ONE OF THE TWO LIGHTS that remained on at Union Bay City News was snuffed out as a woman got to her feet. Slinging her laptop bag over her shoulder, she left her cubicle, walking around to Mpho. "You should probably go home and get some rest," she rested her arm on Mpho's shoulder and leaned her head against Mpho's. "It's not like we're getting paid overtime for staying behind."

"This morning you said you were surprised the war hadn't started," Mpho stopped typing. "Well, now we're in the middle of it, I'm just doing my job."

Jessica stepped back. "You can't seriously still be covering this Premeditator thing."

"Someone has to do it."

"Wesley is going to kill you."

"Wesley needs to remember that he is an editor, not the writer."

"Yeah, but if he says no, it's no. What are you gonna do?"

"That, I will have to figure out if or when it happens."

"It almost certainly will happen; we both know it. Uyanqena yini ukuvula iblog?"

"Jess, don't even start."

"Goodnight Mpho," she laughed as she headed for the exit. "Don't forget to lock up and go home."

"I'll go home when I feel like it," he watched Jessica walk away, almost like a model down a runway.

"See you tomorrow Mpho," the woman left.

Once again, silence enveloped the office. Mpho considered the next words of his article. Finally finding them, his fingers met the keyboard, each click echoing after the other. At the sound of movement, Mpho stopped. "Jess?" he got to his feet, glancing around. He returned to his seat and continued typing. Again, the sound of shuffling stopped him. This time, he remained silent. His eyes darted around the office. Slowly, he closed his laptop, bagged it then clicked off the table light. Leaving everything but his laptop bag, Mpho scurred towards the exit. He couldn't help feeling anxious about being at the office by himself tonight, it was better to finish the article in the comfort of his home he thought. A sweeping shadow caught his eye. He ducked. Heart thumping. Breathing heavy. He pulled out his phone and dialled a number he had memorised years ago. Reducing the volume, he placed the phone to his ear and listened to it ring.

"*Mpho?*"

"Mel, hi. I'm sorry to call you so late, but you know I wouldn't unless it was important."

The woman on the other end of the line sighed. "*What's wrong?*"

"I need you to take Hayley for a little bit."

"*What did you do?*"

"I'll pick her up tomorrow, there's just something I have to deal with now. I'll explain everything to you later, I just need you to go pick up Hayley right now. I've already paid the sitter, just send her home."

"*I'm almost an hour away.*"

"Please just go fetch her."

"*Okay, fine, I'll be there as soon as I can.*"

"Thank you. Let me know once she's with you," Mpho ended the call and pocketed his phone. Lifting his head above the cubicle of his hiding, he couldn't see any shadow moving in the darkness. Securing his bag on his shoulder, he moved slowly, maintaining a crouched posture as he took deliberate steps towards the door. Each step steady. Each breath heavy. He scurried to the door and grabbed the handle, but as he pulled it open, it swung back at him, knocking his head and dropping him to the ground.

The rest of the door opened, revealing a blurry dark figure looming outside. As the figure stepped into the office, it became more difficult for Mpho to see. He pulled the sling of his bag back onto his shoulder, turned onto his belly, and dragged himself one elbow at a time away from the assailant. Without getting far, his ankle was caught in a tight grip. His heart leapt to his throat. Kicking the hand at his ankle off, he shot up. Adrenaline taking over. He dashed around a cubicle and ducked again. He exhaled. In an attempt to bolt to the editor's office, he was pulled back. His bag was caught on the handle of a chair, almost twisting his shoulder out of place as he hit the ground again.

Once more, the figure loomed above him. Slightly more focused than before, but not enough to make out any demographics. The assailant leaned down, grabbed Mpho's bag, and pulled out the laptop.

"No," the journalist choked.

The assailant lifted the laptop and brought it down hard against the desk. Then repeated the process twice more. The aluminium shattered and rained on Mpho. He turned, covering himself to little effect.

A kick to the stomach forced Mpho to groan, unable to swallow the pain.

"Stop," the assailant finally spoke. "Stop pursuing the Premeditator. Or else... Just stop. Before you get—"

The words were halted by a knock on the back of the assailant's head. Cursing, the assailant turned, left arm swinging and knocking the attacker down.

Jess cried out as she hit the floor.

Mpho was still trying to calm the shaking of his head when he heard a terrifying crackling sound. Looking up, he caught a glimpse of the assailant leaning down with a device in hand. The device touched Jess. Then the crackling repeated. Jessica's body shook as thousands of electrical volts traversed through her nervous system. Still in shock, another jolt was delivered to her.

"No," Mpho stained his arm to reach out and grab the assailant's leg. In agonizing pain, he pulled back.

The person who had attacked him, destroyed his computer and tased his colleague got his turn on the ground. But it wasn't long. Within moments, the assailant was limping away and out of the building.

"Jess, are you okay?" Mpho dragged himself to the side of his colleague, cupped her cheeks and placed his forehead against hers. "Please, stay with me." He pulled his phone out and called his aunt – his mother's sister. As per her routine, she had closed her practice for the day and was working at Union Bay Gen for the night.

"*She's just in a state of shock because tasers target the nervous system, but you say she took two charges?*"

"Yes."

"*Then she definitely needs to come in so we can check her, and make sure she's okay.*" For a moment, the doctor spoke off the phone. Mpho could barely hear her instruct someone to send an ambulance. "*Mpho? You still there?*"

"Yes, ngisakhona."

"*Okay, an ambulance is on the way, just hang tight.*"

THE MINUTES HAD TICKED by in excruciating silence as Mandisa Xaba and Thando Msani tried to filter their way through the lucrative documents that the late business tycoon had kept hidden.

"Mandisa. I think I have something." She grabbed the document she was reading and walked over to the detective. "Maybe it's nothing but UBCB keeps popping up."

"That's not nothing." Mandisa took the document from Thando. "Highlight everywhere it appears on the other documents." She flipped through the papers, scanning the parts that had not been redacted.

Thando highlighted a few documents before one piqued her interest. "Listen to this," she cleared her throat. "Union Bay City Bank. REDACTED to be transferred to REDACTED account on the REDACTED." She skimmed past a few paragraphs, filled with more frustrating redactions than information. "Union Bay City Bank to reverse transaction from REDACTED to REDACTED after the news of the embezzlement."

"Embezzlement?" Mandisa looked around at the documents. After touching a few, she picked one up and flipped to the second of its two pages. "Embezzlement, here." At the end of the document were five signatures. "Do you recognize any of these signatures?" she showed to Thando.

Thando got up and walked around the table to look at the document over Mandisa's shoulder. "The first one is my dad's... was.... The others I don't know." She tilted her head thoughtfully. "But I've seen this one before," she indicated to the last signature. "I can't remember where though."

"Give it some thought."

Thando returned to her seat and continued her search for Union Bay City Bank.

Mandisa pulled her phone out and started searching for articles on embezzlement cases that happened in the city. There weren't many articles on the topic, but those that she could find were too recent to be relevant, given the time of Union Bay City Bank's files from 2012 that Phume had gone through. She opened her Contacts app and scrolled to **Mpho Seme (journalist)**. She stared at the number, her mind jumping back to the last time they spoke.

"*This is not a decision to be taken lightly, it's one there's no coming back from. We can still—*"

"*Get out.*"

She shook the memory off and scrolled further down the contact list, finally stopping at **Zanele Sibisi (informant)**. She got out of her seat, "I'll be right back," she hit the call button and walked into the next room.

After a few rings, a voice, almost a tired whisper, answered, "*Hello?*"

"Zanele, I hope I'm not interrupting."

"*Sorry, who am I speaking to?*"

"Mandisa Xaba."

"*Oh, detective. How can I help you?*"

"I need you to look through some old articles for me."

"*What do you need? I'll check first thing when I get to the office tomorrow.*"

"Actually, it's a bit of an emergency."

"*Detective, it's late.*"

134

Mandisa didn't respond.

Zanele sighed. "*Okay, I'll see what I can find on the website.*"

"I need you to find a post or article about embezzlement from 2012. See if you can find anything that has to do with Union Bay City Bank."

"*And when exactly do you need this information by?*"

"As soon as possible."

The woman groaned. "*I'll see what I can do.*"

"Thank you," she ended the call and walked back into the dining room.

A man just taller than Mandisa was now standing behind Thando's chair, a garment bag resting on his left arm. "Detective," he greeted with a smile.

"Mpumelelo."

"I remember where I know the signature from."

"*You* remembered?" the man asked. "Is that right?"

"Okay, fine, my dearest brother," Thanda indicated to the man standing behind her, "who doesn't like to gloat, reminded me."

"Okay."

"Vihaan Naicker," she said proudly. Then she noticed the detective's expression had no surprise.

"And you know his signature, how?"

"Okay, so whenever we need something from the bank, we deal directly with him. No one else, ever since we moved here back in 2006."

"Are you sure it's his signature?"

Thando grabbed her phone and started scrolling through it, "I can't imagine being wrong about this, it's on so many bank statements. I don't know why I didn't realize it myself. There," she showed the phone to the detective.

Mandisa looked at the cell phone screen then the signed document then back at the screen.

"The other signatures must belong to the other members of the Founding Five," said Thando. "So, it must have been ubaba, Vihaan, the..." she visibly suppressed herself from throwing up. "Kingpin. And Nozizwe."

"No."

"No?"

"Nozizwe wasn't one of them. The lawyer was Mthandazo Makhanya, I saw him on the 2nd, and he admitted he was one of them."

"Wait, the 2nd as in today?" asked Mpumelelo.

The detective looked between the siblings with a questioning gaze. "Yes."

"And here I was thinking I'm the one who's overdue on some well-deserved rest," Mpumelelo remarked. "You, detective, need a vacation."

"I'm fine, but anyway my point is none of these belong to him," she sighed. "Which means, contrary to my first theory, these people who are being attacked are not the Founding Five."

"Then who could the others be?"

"I'm starting to suspect that it's people who had something to do with the 'embezzlement.'"

"Embezzlement?"

"Just over a decade ago, there was a quickly hushed embezzlement. It was settled by someone who was recently killed for it."

"Nozizwe Biyela," Mpumelelo added.

"Yes. But I have a feeling this settlement was more of a do as you're told conversation rather than a mutual agreement."

"You're talking about coercion."

"Yes."

"No."

"I know what it sounds like..."

"No, you have no idea what it sounds like."

"Thando."

"No Mpu. Ubaba did everything by the book, and you know that. He had values and principles. So, excuse me for not wanting to consider your theory detective."

"Thando—"

"I think we're done here. You can take the files and show yourself out." Grabbing her phone from Mandisa, she stormed off.

"Forgive her," Mpumelelo sighed. "Our father is still a bit of a touchy subject in this house."

"I can imagine."

"Can you?"

The detective bowed her head for a moment before responding. "More than you know."

Mpumelelo draped the garment bag on one of the chairs. "I'll help you pack this up."

"You don't have to."

"Then I want to," he forced a smile across his lips. "I'm helping you whether you like it or not. I'd prefer it if it was the former."

"Fine," Mandisa sighed. Together they began organizing the documents in a pile in chronological order. Mandisa's phone vibrated on the table.

Zanele Sibisi (informant).

"You can take it. I'll finish up here," Mpumelelo offered.

Thanking him, the detective answered the call and stepped back into the lobby. "Yeah?"

"I've looked for everything you asked for and it's... weird."

"Weird how?"

"There's a trace of articles from a massive embezzlement case from 2012, however, nothing solid. It's all been deleted, and I don't have the clearance to access files that are in the backup server."

"So, someone was trying to hide it."

"Yeah. Sorry."

"It's okay, you've done enough. Thank you." Pocketing her phone, she turned on her heels. Mpumelelo was holding the file folder in his hand.

"Everything okay?"

"Everything's fine."

"You keep using that word, fine." He stepped closer to the detective. "But I'm not convinced that you're okay," he offered the folder, his eyes darting between Mandisa's eyes and lips.

"Thank you for your help," she stole her own glance at Mpumelelo's lips. "And for your concern," she took a step back and received the folder from him.

"Anytime." He walked the detective out. "I'm sorry to bring this up but, the police are probably all over your house, so if you want to stay here you can. You know we have enough rooms."

"Thank you, but I've organised something already," she lied. Her only plan was to find a safe place to park and sleep in her car. Probably show up at one of her few friend's houses to quickly freshen up and get ready for tomorrow.

Mpumelelo nodded and watched the detective drive off before he headed back into the house.

"You're unbelievable."

Mpumelelo looked up to see his sister at the top of the stairs. "Dadewethu."

"You can't possibly be lusting to get in her pants while you're still sleeping around with that intern of yours."

"Thando."

"Leave me alone," she walked out of sight.

CHAPTER 28

KwaZulu Union Bay City, November 3rd, 2023

FIVE MINUTES TO TEN. The wind had a particularly crispy howl that morning in KwaZulu Union Bay City. The streets were quiet. But the courthouse was buzzing. Packed to the brim, people were shouting at the top of their lungs with various voices climbing over each other.

"Lock him up!"

"Give him a fair trial!"

"Justice!"

"The death punishment!"

"He's an innocent man until proven guilty, what ever happened to a fair trial?"

"He's a murderer!"

"Fair trial for what? For who?"

Along the aisles stood heavily armed unmoving security guards. Media reporters with their small crews squeezed into whatever place they could find.

With every eye, and every camera focused on him, chained at his wrists and ankles, the accused was led into the courtroom. So bound from his hands to his ankles he could only shuffle 3-inch steps at a time. With passive aggression, he was seated at the witness bench. A smirk played on the officer's mouth as he moved to the far wall, his eyes never shifting away from Mandla.

The bailiff assessed the crowd. "Settle down. Settle down!" he yelled. A losing battle. His voice was a drop in the ocean of shouts. Rattled he looked around the courtroom that he'd never seen so packed. Blinking quicker by the second, he could feel bullets of sweat working their way down his face. He couldn't control the rowdy crowd and he felt the nerves working through him until he noticed the relaxed lawyer representing KwaZulu Union Bay City getting to her feet.

Observing her surroundings, the prominent Lihle Maphumulo turned from her table. She was dressed in a tailored black skirt suit with a white trim along the edges. Silence fell upon the crowd as her eyes swept across the courtroom. It was a provincial fact that this was her territory, and everyone in attendance knew it. After a few moments, she turned back to the bailiff and gave him a slight nod.

"Thank you," the bailiff mouthed. After announcing the opening formalities, he said, "All rise. Honourable Judge Nonkululeko Msimang presiding."

The judge's door opened. Her heels clicked on the wood beneath them as she approached her bench. "You may be seated," she lowered herself into her black leather chair.

Organizing her papers in front of her, she narrowed her eyes over the frame of her glasses looking at the accused. She readjusted her glasses as she glanced at her paperwork. "Mandla Magwaza."

The accused got to his feet.

"You are being charged with two counts of murder," lifting her head from the papers in front of her, the judge stopped herself. "Where's your lawyer?"

Mandla got to his feet. "Someone who doesn't care what happens to me, who'll do a half job for a bad pay?" he scoffed. "I don't believe I will be needing one of those today. With, all due... respect," he looked at Lihle.

"This is a serious case Mr Magwaza."

"I'm being accused of murdering two people who I had no relations with. I don't think anyone understands how serious this case is as much as I do."

"For the purpose of the record, I have to ask you, are you sure you do not want a lawyer?"

Mandla sighed audibly. "So he, or she could lose the case without even trying just because he, again, or she believes what everyone else believes regardless of the facts? Again, no, I do not want a lawyer. Because that's the exact problem with the justice system. Rumours, gossip and fiction run the court instead of evidence and factual information, because our police, it seems can't seem to do their jobs right."

"You will treat this court with respect for as long as you are in it, is that clear? Good," she acknowledged Mandla's nod. "Now, how do you plead?"

"Not guilty."

The two words became the spark that lit up a barrage of questions and comments from the gallery. Each voice tried to shout over the next.

"Order, order!" the judge banged her gavel. "Mr Magwaza, you were arrested based on your testimony admitting to killing Nozizwe Biyela and the man who seems to only be known as Mkhonto."

Mandla took a moment to himself as the crowd settled. "With all due respect," he began. "Did I?" he tilted his head. "You see, the problem with educated folks is that they think they're smart, but they're actually the most clueless fools of all." He took another pause letting the surprise of the gallery pass. "The journalist insinuated that I killed them, I just said they deserved it. And I know you agree with me on the latter. And so do many people. That's what brought together this vast crowd of witnesses here today," he stretched his arms as wide as his restraints would allow. "All these people didn't come here to see if I'm innocent or guilty, they're here because they want to see how this story unfolds. That man... the one they called the kingpin. Correct me if I'm wrong, but he crossed so many lines of the law and made such a mockery of our justice system. The police ran in circles for years chasing their tails trying to pin him to even a single one of his operations and yet they still have nothing." He watched as the eyes of the judge, jumped from him to Lihle, to someone in the gallery then back to him. "But then again, you can always tell me that I'm wrong about that."

The judge took off her glasses and looked at Mandla. "Are you done?"

"I am."

"Considering the information Mr Magwaza has given us, I can say that the ball is in your court Mrs Maphumulo."

Lihle rose from her seat, her eyes fixated on Mandla. "Let's skip the unnecessary back and forth, shall we? Unlike yourself Mr Magwaza, I have never been one for theatrics," Lihle explained.

Mandla smirked.

"I was privileged to listen to the recording from your conversation with Mpho Seme, and..." she glanced down a moment. "You're right," she looked at Mandla. "You didn't admit to anything. But that doesn't make you innocent of the crimes you are being charged with. So tell me, Mr Magwaza, what was your last paying job?" Lihle asked.

"Objection, irrelevant," Mandla replied.

"I will have to agree," the judge added.

"Your honour, I assure you Mr Magwaza's past employment will be of particular interest to the case."

The judge narrowed her eyes at Lihle. "It would be great if you got to your point swiftly." She turned to Mandla, "Please answer the question."

"I was employed by RZ Investments."

"That's the investment bank owned by one Mr Robert Zietsman for those who are not aware. How did your time with them come to an end?"

"The contract was terminated."

"For embezzlement, is that right?"

Judge Msimang looked at Lihle, then back at Mandla. "Please answer the question."

"Leading the witness," Mandla replied.

"I don't care, I said answer the question."

Mandla sighed lightly. "Yes."

"After being fired for embezzlement, you were arrested, correct?"

"Yes," he replied through gritted teeth.

"Your first offence. After being released from prison, you did not attempt to find a job."

"Is there a question?"

"Yes. Why didn't you look for employment?"

"Objection, irrelevant."

"The question speaks to your integrity Mr Magwaza, so I assure you sir that it is in your best interest to answer."

"Answer the question Mr Magwaza."

"I did not think I would get employed by anyone after being released."

"Is that the truth, or were you plotting how you will murder the people who put you in prison?"

"Objection, leading the witness," Mandla argued.

"I withdraw my previous statement. Before you were arrested for embezzlement, RZ Investments wasn't going to press charges. But suddenly after you went to the media about Union Bay City Bank, your former employer had you arrested."

"Your honour, she's testifying."

"I'm inclined to agree Mrs Maphumulo. Where are you going with this?" asked the judge.

"Who was the prosecutor on your case of embezzlement Mr Magwaza?"

Mandla starred dangers through the lawyer.

"Mr Magwaza?" said the judge.

Mandla chuckled, "Oh, you're good. You're as good as they say you are. You know who it was."

"I do, but you're not here to answer to me, you're here to answer to the court."

"Mr Magwaza, who was the prosecutor on your case of embezzlement?" the judge asked, her tone harsh.

"Nozizwe Biyela."

Gasps broke out through the crowd. Camera shutters went off throughout the room.

"But why did she have to be the prosecutor? A rather difficult question with a simple answer when you know where to look. This document proves the identity of the man who has been known for years as Mkhonto," she handed a document to the judge and a copy to Mandla. "His blood was traced and found to match that of the child to which that birth certificate belonged to. Mr Magwaza, please read the name on that birth certificate for the court."

"Nduduzo Biyela."

"According to hospital documents, Mr Biyela was the definite older brother of the late Nozizwe Biyela. You killed them both."

"Mrs—"

"I'll rephrase, did you not kill them?" Lihle asked.

"Did I not plead not guilty?" Mandla replied. "That man," he pointed out Mpho. "Came to me with an army, and accused me of murder, when I was nowhere near any of the crime scenes! And according to his article," pointing at Mpho again. "The first body was found by your detective," now shifting his finger to Sithole. "After suspicious activity was reported in the area of this Mkhonto's house. Where was that detective after the second body was found, which was not reported mind you." Mandla took a moment to pause, allowing the audience time to grasp what he had said. "In fact, I think that the better question is where is she now?"

"Mr Magwaza watch yourself," the judge warned.

The captain slowly got to his feet.

"Your detective, captain. Where is your detective? This is on you! You wanted help with your job, here it is. Your detective does whatever she wants, to whoever she wants to, whenever she pleases, and you do nothing, nothing about it."

"Mr Magwaza—"

"Find your detective!"

"I will hold you in contempt."

"You're at fault here captain."

Captain Sithole immediately stormed out, leaving a whirlwind of chaos in the courtroom in the wake of being questioned.

"The blood that flows down our streets is on your hands!"

"Order, order!" the judge banged her gavel. "Take him away!"

"Your hands are red captain," Mandla continued to shout as the bailiff pulled him off the witness stand.

Lihle took her seat as the courtroom erupted into chaos, the judge continuously calling for order, a futile effort as the bailiff escorted Mandla out through the back door.

"Where is he taking him?" Mpho questioned. "Where is he taking him?" he tried to shout over the crowd.

MANDISA'S AUNT, ZINTLE and her husband were watching the trial via the Union Bay Newsroom Live live stream on their television. As chaos ruled over the courtroom, the broadcast cut to the studio, where the presenter, Nolwazi Bhengu, explained that their crew had to get out before things escalated any further.

"Turn it off."

"Everything okay babe?"

"Please, turn it off."

He immediately turned the television off and turned to his wife. "What's wrong?"

Zintle grabbed her phone from the coffee table and scrolled through as quickly as she could.

"Zintle uyangithusa manje."

She continued as if she could not hear a thing. Then she found it. An article titled **Crime Boss Killed In His Home**. She skimmed through the article for the words female, woman and detective. An unsettling feeling turned her stomach as she saw them. There was only one female detective in Captain Sithole's station, and that was her niece. In shock, she covered her mouth.

"Zintle."

"It's Mandisa."

"Mandisa? What's Mandisa."

Zintle looked at her husband. "The detective he was talking about." She scrolled through her contact list to her niece's number. After a moment of hesitation, she hit the call button. It rang a few times before it was answered.

"*Molo. Makazi. Hello?*"

"Ma— Mandisa."

"*Aunt Zintle, is everything okay?*"

"Yes... uhm, no. It's... no."

"*Aunt Zintle, utheni?*"

"I'm fine, just... where are you?"

A moment passed before she answered. "*I'm at work.*"

"So, you didn't go to the court case?"

"*Hayi, I don't have time for that. Not everyone can take a day off work to watch someone else's life. No offence makazi.*"

"Okay," she nodded. "Okay, so the guy who was killed..."

"*You know I can't talk about active investigations.*"

"Yes, but is it still active if the criminal was caught."

"*Makazi, you have nothing to worry about.*"

"So, you had nothing to do with it?"

"*Nothing to do with what?*"

"The crime boss. The man who was killed on the 1st."

"*Hayi! No,*" she sighed. "*Listen, I have to go. But I had nothing to do with that, okay?*"

"Okay."

"*I'll call you later, I have to go.*"

Zintle remembered that the last time Mandisa said that, she never did call. "Okay. Please be safe."

"*Always.*"

Zintle ended the call with a sigh.

"Wait. Please don't tell me that you... You didn't honestly think...?"

Zintle hung her head in response. With a sigh, her husband enveloped her in his arms.

CHAPTER 29

UNION BAY CITY BANK was empty that afternoon as the sun began to sink behind the cityscape. The CEO had sent home everyone who didn't take "sick leave" to go attend the big Mandla Magwaza vs KwaZulu Union Bay City case. His secretary had insisted on staying, but he shooed her right out of the front door. After which, he returned to his office, rendering him alone in the building. He'd told his wife he'd have a long day at work due to financial year end so as not to wait for him to eat dinner. Piles of organized papers stacked his office as he stood in front of a paper shredder, stuffing as many papers through it as fast as humanly possible. A knock on the door made him jump, and fumble the papers in his hands.

"Didn't mean to scare you," Mandisa explained as she stepped into the office.

"Yeah, right. I'm sure you didn't," the CEO sighed. "How'd you even get in here?"

"You have friends in high places, I have friends in many places." The detective manoeuvred around the piles of paper to get to Vihaan's table.

"You're that detective that found the body."

"I am. It looks like you're running a little low on staff."

"It's Friday, they got an early day."

Mandisa could tell the CEO was not happy to see her. "How generous."

"How can I help you, detective?"

"I was hoping I could help you."

"How so?"

"I was hoping the documents you're destroying aren't copies of these," she indicated to the documents she was holding.

"What is that?"

"Police might say it's evidence, criminals might call it blackmail documents. I consider it incriminating evidence stored for blackmailing on a rainy day."

"Detective, I could have you arrested for breaking and entering."

"Hayi, you can't," she flashed the employee key card she used to enter the building.

"I could have you arrested for theft and trespassing."

"Trespassing would be a reach, but theft is just ridiculous. But even if you could have me arrested. I don't think you would."

"And why is that?"

"Because if these statements are found in my possession, well... let's just say I wouldn't be the only one who needs a lawyer tonight." She could see Vihaan clench his jaw, obviously feeling threatened. "You and I have a common enemy here... Banker." She saw him swallow nervously. "That's what the Founding Five used to call you, neh?"

Vihaan shifted uncomfortably.

"You see, I had an interesting conversation today with... the Lawyer after I had these account records checked. It turns out people are quite talkative when you have something that could put them in prison."

"Okay, just... just think about this for a minute, okay? We can make this go away, all of it. Just tell me what you want?" the CEO pleaded.

"I want equality in workplaces, social spaces, and in homes. I want women to be as respected as men are for their contributions to society. I want fair pay and job opportunities. I want the possibility of employment for women to be based on qualification and experience rather than beauty and body," the detective explained. "Kodwa sobabini siyayazi inintsi lento endiyicelayo."

"I don't understand what you're saying."

"I want justice. This person they call the Premeditator has stained my reputation. I am wanted for crimes I didn't commit. A vigilante is terrorising the city, creating doubt in the police force. And you... are one part of Frankenstein. Your monster is angry and it's picking all of you off one by one." She took a step forward. "So, tell me what happened."

"So you could arrest me?"

"If I do that, I'd be arrested myself, so no, I won't arrest you."

The CEO pulled his chair out and settled into it. "You might want to take a seat," he sighed.

"I'm okay standing," Mandisa replied.

Vihaan nodded. "The past has caught up to us."

"It has a funny way of doing that," she thought back to her conversation with her aunt. She hadn't given much thought to it. However, trying to solve this case – which was pointing to the past at every turn – was starting to get to her. She was starting to understand that you could run from anything and everything, except your past. She had to face her own at some point in time. She shook the feeling off, she had to focus on whatever Vihaan was about to reveal.

"Just over ten years ago, Mandla discovered some... truths, about the founding of the city. Truths that could cause trouble for some very powerful people. People with very deep pockets."

"Yourself included."

Vihaan didn't answer, which gave the detective the answer she needed. "Let's just say these people always get what they want. They could make things happen with just a phone call. At the time, Mandla Magwaza was working for the investor so... He was framed for embezzling money from the company through UBCB, then he was fired," Vihaan hung his head.

"What Lihle Maphumulo said this morning... was it true?"

"Which part?"

"About Mandla being arrested because he went to the media?"

"Yes. But it wasn't supposed to be this way."

"You ruined a man's life. You don't just walk away from that," Mandisa shook her head.

"You have to understand. I didn't want to do it, I didn't want any of this, but I was outvoted," Vihaan pleaded. "Four to one. I had no choice."

"You always have a choice. Whether good or bad, those choices have consequences, and you have to face them, like it or not. The five of you created a killer so your blood is on your own hands," the detective explained. "You did nothing for him back then so you think helping him now will wipe all the guilt and regret away, but it won't."

"I don't know what you're talking—"

"Don't insult my intelligence," Mandisa interrupted. "From what I hear, Mandla didn't just walk out of court this morning, he was escorted out by a cop. My colleagues are a lot of things but corrupt is not one of them. Which means someone was threatening them or knew they were in trouble and offered an easy way out."

"What does that have to do with me?"

"Information is power, but money is control. And judging from the documents you were destroying when I walked in, I'd say Mandla got to you, so you got to a cop."

"You have no evidence of that if it were even true."

"Maybe, but would you like to tell me what happened to your leg? Because I can't imagine that stain is from beetroot."

"I hurt it while I was working in the garden yesterday. Some thorns from my roses cut me."

"Luxoki obu, try again."

"Please. I have a family."

"So did Mandla," Mandisa exclaimed.

A tense silence hovered in the room as the CEO buried his head in his hands. From a distance, the sound of sirens began to ring. Surprised, Vihaan lifted his head to look the detective in the eyes, his own getting watery.

"Please, just let me go. I'll take my family and we'll leave the country. We'll go anywhere, you can decide, all you need to do is say the word and I'm gone."

Mandisa returned Vihaan's gaze, her eyes explaining her disinterest in the offer. "I'm a lot of things Mr Naicker, but I'm not someone who can be bought."

"I'm not going to jail."

"You don't have a choice."

"Like you said, 'You always have a choice.'" He pulled his drawer open and injected himself with the syringe that arrived in the envelope yesterday.

Mandisa's eyes popped open, and she started to rush to the other side of the table but stopped herself as the CEO slowly fell from his chair to the ground. His body started twitching as his veins started to show on his neck.

CHAPTER 30

THE SIRENS ONLY GOT louder as the seconds passed. Mandisa was still shell-shocked by the CEO's act. Gathering herself, she picked up the documents she had walked in with which had since fallen from her grip. With a final glance at Vihaan's helpless face peaking from the side of the table, his eyes were now seeming obscure. Mandisa fled from the office, rushing down the staircase and out the back door into an alley. She knew there wasn't a camera in the area, so she took a moment to yourself. Thoughts of how she's the reason Vihaan killed himself flooded her mind like a wave crashing after another.

TYRES SCREECHED AS police cruisers stopped in front of the Union Bay City Bank building. Police officers flooded onto the street like ants from an anthill. Guns drawn; they approached the main building door. A single officer tested the handle before declaring, "Locked." Detective Thabiso Simelane fired three sets of two bullets in a triangular shape from one top corner to the other then ending at the bottom centre of the glass door. With the side of his fist, he struck the door as high as he could and then covered his head from the falling glass. Officers moved around him to enter the building, jumped over the key card checkpoint and assumed a C formation in the foyer.

"Our guy is on the thirty-eighth floor, corner office. Team beta, up the stairs, team alpha is in and on the elevator, let's move!" Thabiso instructed.

Many officers diverged to the staircase as Thabiso led a smaller team to the elevators. The elevator doors dinged open. The officers walked in, four in each of the two elevators. Thabiso pressed for floor 37. As soon as the door closed, an officer gave Thabiso a boost and he opened the top hatch of the elevator. As it continued to speed up the building, Thabiso and another officer climbed out and closed the hatch. After a few moments, the elevator stopped. Thabiso looked at the officers on top of the other elevator and nodded. Together the two officers opened the door to the 38th floor, Thabiso and his partner jumped over to the other elevator and rushed onto the 38th floor, not long after followed by the two officers. With cautious speed, they approached the well-lit corner office. A side door bolted open, and they turned their attention to it. Team beta walked through. Spotting the detective, the team leader, Jabu, shook his head, there was no one on the staircase. They slowly converged on the office. Thabiso pushed the office door open with his boot and stepped in, his eyes leading his gun around the office before landing on the head peeking from the side of the table. Thabiso approached the table, kicking aside the piles of paper in his way. A whiff of the air told him the story, the target was already dead, and he covered his nose for a moment. Turning back to his team, he ordered, "Search the entire building. Set up a 10-kilometre blockade."

As the quads spread out, the captain stepped into the office to find Thabiso examining the body on the ground. The detective looked up to Sithole and shook his head. The captain instructed the CSI he arrived with to check the door for fingerprints.

Within ten minutes, all units had returned from their sweep of the building with nothing to show.

The CSI, however, had just finished processing and re-entered the office to present her results to the captain. "Sir. We have a match on the prints."

"Okay, spit it out."

The CSI swallowed. "It's... it's one of our own. Detective Mandisa Xaba."

The captain sighed as he rubbed his eyes and pinched the bridge of his nose. "You're sure?"

"One hundred per cent."

"Put out an APB for the arrest of Mandisa Xaba," he instructed Jabu. "I want her brought in alive," he looked at Thabiso. "Alive," he repeated. He turned to the CSI, "Pull his blood and find out what chemical that thing sticking in his arm had."

A ping went off in Thabiso's pocket.

"Sorry about that," he said as he pulled his phone out of his pocket to silence it. But before he was able to do so another ping went off. This time from the captain, followed by another on the table.

The captain pulled out his phone and fury filled his eyes as his fingers strangled the device.

Ladies and Gentlemen of KwaZulu Union Bay City. I must thank you for your time and participation over this week. However, like good things, everything must come to an end. Receive this final riddle with my sincere gratitude. When the rich get richer so do I. I play because I can't lose, I don't lose because I cheat, what am I? Solve the riddle and save a life. You have five hours.

When the captain lifted his head, he found all eyes were on him. He took a moment to look around. "Okay, listen up. We may have Xaba's prints that put her on the scene, but we don't actually know what happened here. So, we find Xaba, and we bring her in. Nothing more, and nothing less. We bring her in alive, or not at all."

Some of the officers glanced at Thabiso then returned their attention to the captain.

"You have your orders, let's move."

"Captain," Thabiso called out. "What if she resists?" he questioned.

Again, the Captain took a glance around. "As a last resort, shoot to kill," he instructed.

CHAPTER 31

IN A QUIET SUBURBAN neighbourhood, a peach-painted house stood out in the dimming of the evening light. The small garden at the edge of the property was well maintained. The glass was recently cut. The journalist's house. Inside, the television was on in the living room. The journalist was seated on the couch, a young girl resting in his embrace, her head lazily on his shoulder. Lights flooded through the window as a car turned into the driveway and then turned off. The roaring of the engine outside slowed before going silent. Looking down, Mpho realized his baby girl had fallen asleep. Gently, he picked her up and carried her to her room, tucked her into bed and kissed her forehead. As he turned, the small hand of the child wrapped around Mpho's wrist.

"Daddy?"

"Yes baby."

"Goodnight."

"Goodnight Hayley," he kissed her forehead again. Leaving the room, he closed the door with utmost care. His heart beating a little faster than it was before. Slowly placing one foot in front of the other, he returned to the living room, switched off the light and slowly drew back a bit of the curtain. He could feel his throat tighten as he saw the car in his driveway, he didn't recognize it. As Mpho peaked a little more through the curtain, he almost jumped as a shadowy figure walked past the window. His breathing got heavier. Then a knock on the door. Too frightened to approach the door, he just stood there, staring at the thick wooden door. Vibrations reverberated from the sofa as his phone began to ring. With caution, he looked over the sofa.

Detective Xaba lit his phone. He sighed and then answered it.

"Vula umnyango, we have to talk," the detective demanded.

Relief washed over Mpho as he exhaled.

"Mpho, open the door."

"Okay, okay, I'm... I'm coming." His heart finally slowed down as he opened the front door.

"Naicker is dead," the detective announced as she let herself in.

"What?"

"Uswelekile."

"Uswelekile? That means died, right?"

"Dead. Uzibulele, and now they think it's me," she began as she paced the living room.

"Keep it down, Hayley just went to sleep. Hold on a second, why would they think it was you?"

"Because I was there. I was there in his office."

"But you're a detective, you're used to seeing that."

"I've seen bodies, but I've never seen anyone kill themself!"

"Keep it down," Mpho pleaded. "But what happened? What were you doing in his office?"

"Umsebenzi wam."

"That's a fair answer."

"He killed himself in front of me," her eyes got teary as she stopped pacing.

"Are you hurt?"

"Hayi," she rubbed the back of her head. "He used some injection."

"Okay, that's good. Well, it's not good that he's dead but you're okay so that's... that's good."

"I am not okay."

"Look, at the bank they have cameras right? So, when the police, or your colleagues rather, see the footage, then they will know that it wasn't you who, you know..." he gestured a small cut along his neck, making a low growl in his throat.

"There is no footage."

"What do you mean there's no footage? There's like a thousand cameras in that building, at least one of them has to work."

"On the scanners, they said the cameras stopped recording before I arrived."

"That doesn't make any sense, who would stop the cameras from recording?"

"The only person in the building."

"Vihaan? But why?"

"I caught him destroying dozens of documents. So, he obviously didn't want any evidence of himself destroying more evidence that could get him arrested."

"Let me get you a glass of water."

"Andifuni amanzi. I need to know what injection Naicker used, where he got it from and when."

"We'll get to—"

"That's three people," Mandisa interrupted. "He has killed three people and walked away to who knows where.

"Now he's going for the fourth."

"Uthini?"

"Didn't you get the message?"

"What message?"

"From... from the Premeditator. It's blowing up all over social media." Mpho grabbed his phone and after a few swipes on the screen, he handed it to Mandisa.

Her eyes ran across the screen. "When you say it's blowing up, which platforms are you referring to?"

"More like which am I not? It's all over the place, everyone is talking about it. I had to mute the work group because journalists don't shut up when they catch wind of a story the police have no control over. All the attention that the Premeditator wanted, he finally has it. Everyone is trembling in fear and it's not just in the city, this has made its way up the food chain from the mayor to the minister of defence, and likely the president. People want answers. The international attention isn't helping either."

"Forget this," she handed the phone back to Mpho. "We need to figure out who the next victim is cause I'm getting really tired of running from the police while chasing around this sociopath's riddles."

"Okay, what did you get from..." he swallowed.

"Not much that we didn't already know from the information Mthandazo gave us, and also from Maphumulo's insinuations in court."

"You were there?"

"No, I saw the videos." She started pacing around the coffee table. "It seems like lawyers are the only people who actually have a clue of what's going on in the grander scheme of things."

"Could you stop pacing, please."

"Helps me think."

"Okay..." Mpho shook his head. "So, what now?" he questioned.

"Let's look at what we know."

"He likes his riddles."

"Important information Mpho."

"He's checking out some powerful people."

"He calls himself the broker which means he has some kind of power."

"Information?"

"Exactly," Mandisa confirmed.

"We also know that he's tech-savvy and has a wide reach."

"Has access to any facility he wants, residential and workplaces."

"Wants to be seen, probably from a lack of mommy's attention growing up."

"No," she eyed Mpho. "That's where his M.O. gets contradictory. He knows how to stay under the radar."

"He knows how to kill and he's not afraid to execute."

Mandisa stopped pacing.

"You have an idea?" Mpho's eyes lit up.

The detective thought back to the financial books of Union Bay City Bank and what Phume explained to her "This money wasn't embezzled, it was just... shifted around to make it seem that way." Her eyes narrowed as she remembered the redacted files from Zenzele's safe. "He wants to be seen..."

"That's what I said."

"You might be onto something."

"Well, I mean he's only killed three people like you said."

"No, about wanting to be seen. Maybe it's not about being seen," Mandisa insinuated. "Maybe it's about acknowledgement."

"Okay, you've lost me."

"He's not just going after people of power, he's exposing the people who ruined his career, reputation and life. Some of which just so happen to be part of the Founding Five."

"And how do you know that?"

"Naicker."

"I thought you said you didn't get much from him. Mandisa, that's much. When were you going to share that information?"

Mandisa lifted her head to face the journalist.

"You weren't going to, were you? Mandisa this is serious."

"You think I don't know that? He's killed some of the most powerful people in Union Bay. People who could make you go away without thinking twice. Have you considered what would happen if he missed one of them and they retaliated? What would happen if they wanted to shut you up? There are some things I couldn't tell you for your own safety. And your daughter's."

"Don't... don't you dare bring her into this."

"What has happened has happened. We can't undo it."

"These people. They obviously had secrets. The question is what are they? What is it that he knows that they don't want in the public eye?"

"It doesn't matter, let's go."

"Oh, is that your way of saying, 'I have more information I'm not going to tell you?'"

"Mpho, masambe."

"To where?"

"Robert Zietsman." Mandisa opened the front door and waited for the journalist. "He's the last target."

"What if it's not him?"

"It is."

"Well, I can't just leave Hayley, and Mel."

"Who's Mel?

"Her mother."

"They're both here, problem solved."

"No, problem not solved. It's not safe to leave them alone. If it was your child, would you not want to make sure she's safe?"

The detective sighed, regret for asking washed over her. "You have somewhere they can go?"

"Yeah, I have family they can go to, but it's getting late, it's probably not a good idea to disturb—"

"Thank you for the excess of information," Mandisa interrupted. "Get Hayley and Mel... you'll drop them off with... whoever after you leave me at Zietsman's. You do have a license, right?"

"Of course, I do."

"If I'm going to drop you off at the place, why do you need me?"

"Because we're going to need your contacts."

"I knew working with you would create problems for me," Mpho sighed. He grabbed his phone and after a moment placed it to his ear. "Hey, I hope I'm not disturbing." He paused for a moment, allowing the person on the other end of the line to answer. "Where are you right now?" he said as he disappeared into the hallway.

Not long after, in the double-storey glass mansion, Robert Zietsman lounged on his single-seater sofa, a glass of whiskey in hand. His ears focused on the ticking of the clock behind him. As his head was lifted, downing the rest of his beverage, he noticed a figure looming over him. Without enough time to swallow, a rope looped his neck, forcing the golden liquid out through his gritted teeth. He tried to reach behind himself in an attempt to claw at his assailant. A futile effort. He kept trying till his arms fumbled, and his vision blurred into darkness as he drifted.

CHAPTER 32

BOUND TO A CHAIR BY a well-tied rope, Robert was woken up by the splash of ice and water. Panting in panic, he shook his head. He winced, still feeling the effects of the rope around his neck. He was in his garage. A bright light shone in his direction. His feet were submerged in water, two cables he could not identify due to barely being able to open his eyes were submerged with his feet.

"I catch you at a bad time?" the assailant asked from behind the beaming light. The voice was assertive.

"Listen to me..." he stopped to catch his breath. "We can make a deal."

"I'm not here to cut deals. That's how you always avoid prison, isn't it? It's your way of cheating justice. Cheating the law. You've done that for long enough."

"What do you want? Name your price."

"I have no price. It's time for you to confess to your sins, investor."

"My sins?"

"What you, Msani, Naicker, and the two Biyela's did eleven years ago."

"I don't know what you're talking about."

"I was hoping you'd say that."

Silence replaced their voices. Then electricity jolted Robert's body. The cables next to his feet were jumper cables he finally realized as his breathing steadied.

"Do you recall what I'm talking about now?"

"I have an idea," he grudgingly replied.

He groaned again as the electricity pulsed through his body. This time for double the previous duration. His breathing got heavy when the wave of shock washed over him.

"I..." his breath hitched. "I couldn't stop them. When they found out that it was my employee who uncovered incriminating information on them, they were furious," he explained, his voice trembling. "They wanted to rain all hell. I tried... I tried to stop them, but I couldn't."

"Wrong answer."

Another jolt of electricity travelled through Robert. "You must be enjoying this."

"I wouldn't say that, but you won't hear me complaining either." A few moments passed before the voice spoke again. "Let's try again, shall we?"

Robert sighed. "Seven years. It took seven years to build this city. Can you believe that?"

"Ewe. Seven years to build a city. Seven seconds to build a lie. Seven minutes to destroy a man's life. Seven hours to bring the city to its knees. Life is ironic, isn't it?"

"Everyone you killed. They did nothing wrong. They were innocent, you know that?"

"You said they wanted to rain hell, now you say they did nothing wrong. Which one is it?"

Another jolt. "It was my decision; they were backing my play."

"Why?"

"Because if I went down, everyone would've gone down. You take away the money man, he gets replaced, you take the lawyer, and someone else takes their place. But you remove the money mover, the whole operation sinks with them."

"And what exactly makes the money mover so special?"

"For the love of money is the root of all evil."

"One Timothy six verse... ten."

"Yeah, whatever. Anyone can be the money mover; the problem comes when the money gets larger and larger. Huge sums are hard to track when they're broken into small portions. I'm sure you've heard the story of the one Rand thief. Finding a mover is easy, finding a mover you can trust is neigh impossible. So, replacing the one you have is not much of an option."

"So, the life of a civilian is worth less than the lives of five very powerful people?"

"Oh, how so far you are from understanding the true politics that govern this city. There is no need to draw this out any longer than it needs to be. Do what you must." Before his assailant could respond, a knock came from the front door. Robert could almost feel the glare of his attacker from behind the light.

"You're not gonna do anything stupid while I'm gone, will you?"

"I wouldn't dream of it."

In the seconds of opening and shutting the door that connects the house to the garage, Robert was able to see a trace of his attacker. He waited a moment. "Help! Help me! I'm in the garage," he continued shouting.

The door swung open, the footsteps approaching him heavy on their steps. The light was turned away from Robert and he felt a fist punch into his stomach a moment later. He winced.

"So much for trust."

The sound of glass breaking echoed through the house. Followed by the rushing of feet. Then the ring of a phone in the garage. The feet stopped for a moment, then continued their approach. A cell phone flash swam across the garage, illuminating the two figures in it. Robert's head had slumped.

With a gasp a new voice spoke. "Mandisa? What did you do?"

CHAPTER 33

IN DEAFENING SILENCE, Mpho glared at the detective he had helped for the past two days. After everything that had happened since he met her, he was feeling anxiety and fear begin to creep in. He swallowed the thought. "What did you do?"

The detective looked from Mpho to Robert, her breathing picking up. She followed the jumper cables from Robert's feet to his car. "I... It's not what you think," she spun around to face Mpho.

"It's not what I think? Not what I think as in not what it looks like? Because it looks like you've been torturing him!"

"It's not that simple."

"The hell it is."

"Let's talk in the living room."

"After you," Mpho exhaled heavily.

Slightly hesitant, Mandisa led the way to the dining room. Seeing the laptop on the table she said, "Thanks for remembering my laptop."

"Don't try to change the subject." He placed Mandisa's car keys on the table.

Mandisa nodded as they sat across from each other.

"When you said you'll convince him to confess, this is what you meant? Mandisa what the hell happened when I left you?"

The detective shook her head as she tried to recollect her last memory. "What day is it?"

"Mandisa, this is not a joke."

"I'm serious."

"It's Friday, the 3rd."

The detective exhaled heavily. The last thing she remembered was parking at the mall, writing an update in her diary, and going to sleep after returning from the Msani mansion.

"Mandisa—"

She hesitated, but she knew the only way out of the conversation was through. And the only way through was the truth. Mpho's gaze remained on her as she looked up. "I have... I have D.I.D."

"What's D.I.D?"

"Dissociative Identity Disorder."

"What does that mean?"

Mandisa paused, unable to keep explaining. She could feel her stomach turn the wrong way around. The secret she had kept for close to a decade, she was now explaining to a man she'd known for barely half a week. She ran her hands over her eyes with a sigh. "It..." she choked. "It means I have multiple personalities. So sometimes I blackout for a few minutes, or a few hours. When I wake up, I have no recollection of what I did or said that entire time. It's something I have no control over. And it's haunted me for nine years. I lost friends because of it. I had to seclude myself from my family because of it. I can't even be trusted by my colleagues because of it. And it's made me my greatest fear, and my biggest enemy."

"I- I'm sorry."

Did you kill my mother? Did you abuse me as a child? She thought of asking. She sighed, settling with, "It's not your fault." What she was feeling was a blend of emotions she didn't experience much while on a job. But everything that had led her to this point was piling up on her conscious. The man she beat while undercover a few days ago, not being able to save the Kingpin, the Lawyer, and possibly the Banker too she thought. And never visiting her mother's... She froze in thought before she was able to speak again. "I'm sorry about all of this."

"What are you talking about?"

"This case, this... mayhem. I dragged you into all of this. I shouldn't have asked for your help or mentioned your daughter. I'm sorry."

"This is not your fault. I chose this case as much as you did. When I published that article, I joined the battle. You didn't pull me into this war, I signed up for it. And I knew what I was doing. So, believe me when I tell you..." he searched for Mandisa's eyes, "Hey look at me. Believe me when I tell you that you jumped into the fire and I followed you, and I knew the risk. Sometimes..." he sighed. "Sometimes in life what we do is much bigger than who we are. And the impact that it carries will go far beyond what we can imagine. I chose this. Okay?"

Mandisa nodded and blinked away the tears that were welling up in her eyes. "Okay." She wiped away any strayed tears and composed herself.

"You gonna be alright?"

Mandisa considered the question for a moment. "Yeah," she replied, though truly she was not sure.

Mpho placed his hand over Mandisa's hand, "Hey." She looked at him. "I'm—"

A scream from the garage cut him off.

Mandisa slipped her hand away and got up. "We have to get him to confess."

"Mandisa—"

"Be ready to call Mandla. I'll be right back."

Mpho sighed as the detective walked back to the garage. She ran her hand on the wall next to the door till she found the switch. She flipped it on.

Robert's eyes took a moment to adjust to the fluorescent as he turned to the door. "You're not Mandla. You're that cop. The police are trespassing and torturing now?"

Mandisa looked at him blankly. She didn't know how her other half treated him but thought it good to try and keep whatever impression she made. "Well, I'm not exactly in popular demand back at the station right now," she replied, pulling her gun out as she approached him.

"From what I hear, you're the most wanted woman in the city. You can drop your gun, after everything you put me through, you don't need it to scare me. You've already shown me that you're willing to torture me to the brink of death. And considering you killed the banker; I figured it was only a matter of time before you came for me."

Mandisa's lips parted at the revelation. Composing herself, she closed her mouth. There was no way she could've killed Vihaan she thought to herself. She was many things, but a killer was not one of them. She'd mostly used her gun for show, just as all cops did. It was rare to ever have to discharge it. Regardless, she couldn't deny killing the banker because she didn't know how much Robert knew that she didn't know.

Mpho slipped in. "Everything okay?"

"Yeah," she glanced over her shoulder before turning back to Robert. "I'm going to untie you. Then we'll go to the dining room. I think by now you should be convinced to tell the truth." Holstering her gun, she got to work untying the rope that bound Robert.

"How'd you figure it out?"

"Figure what out?"

"That I was the last of the five."

Mandisa's head shot up in Mpho's direction, her eyes wild.

"I don't think she's the one who has to explain herself," said Mpho. "I'm just intrigued is all."

Mandisa pulled the last rope off Robert and then got back up. "It was just a matter of connecting the dots."

"Those dots being?"

"Everything Lihle Maphumulo said in court," the journalist replied. "But she still couldn't prove anything."

"True, but she created reasonable doubt."

"Let's go. The dining room," Mandisa instructed.

"I'm not sure you'll want to be here when Mandla arrives."

"What makes you think he'll come?"

"This is personal. Why else leave me for last."

Mandisa and Mpho shared a hesitant look.

"Make the call." Mandisa flipped her laptop open and started working it after entering the password.

"Are we sure about this?" Mpho replied. "He's not exactly the most reliable speaker right now."

"No. But at this point, we don't have many options and we're running out of time."

The journalist pulled out his phone and looked at it for a moment. The blank screen reflected him like a dark mirror. Mandisa could only guess what fearful thoughts were consuming him.

"When he answers, he's going to want to get straight to the point, but I need you to control the situation. Drag the call as long as you can."

"So that you can track the call, I know," he nodded. Mpho swiped on the screen a few times before placing the phone on the coffee table. It rang out loud. Mandisa glanced at the clock, the seconds dragged on.

"*Journalist*," a voice came through the small speaker of the mobile device. Mandla's voice was no longer disguised the way it was when he was giving the riddles on air.

"You wanna tell me how you got an escort to freedom?"

"*Not particularly, no.*"

Mpho muted the call. "His voice."

"I know, keep going."

With a sigh, he unmuted. "You know, I just find it funny that—"

"*What do you want?*"

Mpho looked at the detective. "We know who your next target is," he began again. "We have him right here."

"*Is that so?*"

"He's willing to admit to what he did."

"*I already know what he did. It is not I, but the good people, the innocent people of KwaZulu Union Bay that he has to apologize to.*"

"I'm not sure I understand what you're asking."

"*Come on now, you're smarter than that. Or at least you should be. Put it on the news.*"

Robert scoffed.

"I don't think we can do that," said Mpho.

"*Is that you speaking, or is it the detective?*"

Mpho looked to Mandisa who just nodded at him.

"*Tell me, detective, what is the consequence of knowledge?*"

The detective looked away from Mpho and took a moment to consider the question. "The burden of regret," she responded.

"*Right you are.*"

"It's going to take some time to put together the equipment."

"*Oh detective, my dear partner in this beautifully orchestrated crime. You will find I'm a patient man. I've been waiting years for this, what's a few minutes gonna cost? Except the investor's life of course.*"

"We just need a little bit of time."

"*And time you have. However, according to my clock, you have about an hour and twenty minutes,*" and with that, the line went dead.

"Did you get it?"

"Missing the last number."

"What? How does that work?"

"I've been blocked from accessing the police systems and databases, so I had to use this other system, it's..." illegal, she thought. "Stupid," she said. "But it could only be one of ten numbers, so it won't cause much of a problem, it just means I need more time."

"Are you sure it's a good idea to post this?"

"It's a horrible idea, but it's not like we have much of a choice," Robert interjected. "I think that's what you were going to say."

"Actually, I was going to say it's your decision to make."

"It's really not much of an option," Robert responded.

"Not you," she looked at the journalist.

After a moment Mpho sighed. "What's the plan?"

"We'll post it on the Union Bay City News website."

"I could lose my job."

"I could lose my life."

"You're not part of this conversation," the detective indicated to Robert. She turned to Mpho again, "You risked your life for me. It's time I return the favour. Whatever you decide, I'm with you."

"Oh, you chose a really bad time to be nice," Mpho replied. "Ah, forget it. I'm likely to lose my job anyway. I know an anchor from UB Newsroom Live, I'll have to cash in a favour for her to bring the tech though."

"Do it, she has thirty minutes to get here."

"Okay."

"Mpho. She is the only person allowed through that door," Mandisa emphasized.

"One person, got it," he bolted away with his phone in hand.

"Just out of curiosity, how much are you getting paid for all this trouble."

"Whenever you find a moment convenient to you, just don't speak."

"I'm just asking cause—"

"You are not cheating justice this time." Mandisa sat behind her computer and got to work locating the first of ten cell phone numbers.

"Instead of trying to locate all the numbers, why not call them so you know which is the right one, that way you'll only have to locate the one."

"Your profession requires facts and figures, right?"

"Yes."

"So tell me, what's the likelihood of ten people answering the phone in the next two minutes?"

"That's not really the type of thing I have to work out."

"And what do you think will happen if Mandla answers the phone?"

"Well..."

"You hadn't thought that far yet, had you? Now please, shut up."

MANDLA MAGWAZA STARED at his screen, without audio in the dark room. The 28-inch was split into four frames, each frame a camera at a different location. The first frame showed the outside of an old burnt warehouse, it was quiet. The second was bustling with activity from a bird's eye view of the KwaZulu Union Bay City police station. The third was a feed alternating between cameras surrounding Robert's house. The last frame showed the laptop's view of Mandisa as she worked on it.

Mandla picked up his phone and dialled a number. He put the phone to his ear and watched the screen. In the second frame, Captain Sithole checked his ringing phone. He hesitated then answered.

Feigning a concerned voice, Mandla began, "Is- is this the captain of the police station?"

"Yes, how can I help you?"

"You're searching for the rogue detective, right?"

"She's a person of interest, yes. Have you seen her?"

"I think I know who the next victim is."

CHAPTER 34

THE DETECTIVE WAS HARD at work trying to find the location of each of the ten numbers consisting of the same nine digits with only the last number being different. She had started with the number ending with 0 and worked her way up. The first four were unsuccessful, the first was in Cape Town, the second in Amanzimtoti, the third somewhere in Libalele and the fourth in Kimberly. It was the fifth that came closest, St Lucia. The search continued for the detective.

Over in the kitchen, Robert was busy fixing himself a peanut butter sandwich on the island counter. He turned to the microwave. **19:17.** He sighed.

There was a knock on the door. This time it was answered by the journalist. "Nolwazi Bhengu, the people's favourite presenter."

"Flattery is a dangerous game Mpho. And also, it won't butter me up."

"Thanks for coming," he smiled.

"I've been waiting for this day, I hate having 'you owe me's' hanging over my head," the anchor explained. "But I have to say, I wasn't expecting you to cash in via, whatever this is."

"It's a bit of a pickle, isn't it."

"Well, you never could stop chasing danger," Nolwazi exclaimed.

"It's more like it chases me," Mpho replied. "Follow me," he led Nolwazi to the living room. "Mandisa."

"Almost done locating the numbers. Only three are showing promise so far. But I'll still have to triangulate them."

"Mandisa."

"Yes," the detective looked up. She snapped her finger at the anchor, "I know you."

"Nolwazi Bhengu," the anchor introduced herself. "Union Bay Newsroom Live presenter." She held her hand out.

Mandisa shook it. "Do you have the equipment?"

"It's in the van," Nolwazi replied.

"I'll get it and set up just now."

"Okay, then please get her up to speed with the situation."

"Uhm... how much of the situation?"

"All of it."

"Are you sure?"

Mandisa nodded.

"Will do. You're going to love this story."

Mandisa immediately got back to work on her computer, her fingers flying over the keyboard. The final number was non-existent. The detective sighed.

"You look like you need this more than me," Robert remarked as he entered the room, carrying his sandwich in one hand and a cup of coffee in the other.

"Don't take this the wrong way but I don't trust you," Mandisa replied without looking up.

"Oh, come on. What reason would I have to drug you?"

"I said nothing about drugging me, but you did just finish two bottles of whiskey."

"You make a good point," he took a seat. "However, I did just drink a home remedy for hangovers, so I'll be fine in a few."

"You do realize that you're not hungover, right?"

"Yes, I'm not stupid. But they say prevention is better than cure, right?"

"Touché. If you're looking for something to do, you could help Mpho set up the camera equipment."

"I think I'll pass on that." He glanced at the clock. "Forty minutes."

"You're not helping."

"Well, it's not like there's a psychopath out there who wants my blood or anything."

Mandisa took a moment from the screen to look at Robert. Without a word, he stood up and left the room. The detective started triangulating the first of the three most likely numbers.

CHAPTER 35

19:34. Mpho was done setting up the camera equipment and moved on to trying to get the audio right while Nolwazi was wiring Robert. Mandisa was watching carefully while her computer was running the program.

"Okay, you're all set up." Mpho put on a pair of headphones. "Say something."

"And please try to act sober," Mandisa suggested.

"Oh-okay. Well, I don't know what to say."

Mpho adjusted some knobs on the audio machine. "Just practice what you will be saying."

Robert took a deep breath and released it. Then repeated the process twice. He looked into the camera. He clenched his jar; his eyes became daggering. "Eleven years ago, something happened. I would like everyone to know that I am very sorry to have been a part of it and I regret it."

"Okay, cool," Mpho took the headphones off. "We can start."

"That was good, you almost had me convinced," Nolwazi exclaimed.

"Please don't just get straight to the point like that," the detective asked. "At least have the decency to say hello."

Robert nodded.

Mpho walked behind the camera and held his hand up for a countdown. With his free hand, he hit record. "Five, four, three," he continued counting down with his fingers for two and one then pointed at Robert.

"Good evening, ladies and gentlemen. My name is Robert Zietsman. Over a decade ago, Mandla Magwaza, the man you—the man who calls himself the Premeditator, used to work for me. During that time, he came across some confidential information that... that could never see the light of day. The people responsible for the information found out. And I was one of them."

Mandisa turned away, staring into the distance.

"To protect said information, Mandla was framed for embezzlement, and he served time for it. I didn't realize it at first, but after Nozizwe was killed, I knew it was him. I know we shouldn't speak ill of the dead, but Vihaan also knew. He came to me, and he wanted us to flee the country rather than to—"

"Stop," Mandisa yelled.

"Everything okay?"

"Can you hear that?"

"Hear what?" Mpho replied.

"Sirens," the detective answered. "We have to go."

"What?"

"After all my hard work," Robert exclaimed.

"What about the recording?"

"We can't record it from behind bars. Pack the necessities into the van."

"Dismantling everything will take longer than it took setting it up," Mpho explained.

"Maybe we don't need everything," Nolwazi suggested. "Just the camera and sound."

"What are you thinking?"

"We're seven minutes into the evening news, what if we just transmit our feed to UBNL?"

"This is a bad idea," Robert folded his arms.

"We don't have many options." The detective turned to Nolwazi. "Do you know how to do what you're suggesting?"

"Yes, it's a piece of cake, I just have to convince the network to allow it."

"I can't ask you to do this," Mpho expressed.

"And you don't have to."

"Given that we're still here, we may need a distraction when the... the..."

"Police."

"Police get here, yes, thank you. So that we can get away," Robert concluded.

"Or maybe not."

They all turned to Mandisa.

"It's me they want."

"No."

"Yes."

"You can't—"

"Mpho, stop." Mandisa sighed. "You've risked enough. Let me do my job."

"Your job is not to surrender. It's to uphold the law."

"Sometimes you just have to know when to stop."

"And what about Mandla? You'll just let him walk free?"

"I may not like some of my colleagues, but I do have faith that we'll catch him at the end."

"Won't they shoot at you?" the anchor asked.

"They wouldn't dare."

"How could you be sure?"

"They have orders to arrest me on site. If a single trigger goes off, there will be hell. If not from me, from the captain."

"I thought he doesn't like you," Mpho expressed his concern.

"We have our common ground."

"Okay, so we're going through with this insane plan?"

"Yeah."

"What about Mandla?"

"Almost got his location," Mandisa replied. "I'll convince the captain to go there."

"How?"

"I'll find a way. I have to. Nolwazi, make the call to whoever you have to talk to so that you can stream interview style. At this point, it doesn't matter what you have to do, just get it done please."

"Okay."

"Afterwards you can go set up everything needed to stream, Mpho will help you. I have to talk to Robert then he'll be right behind you. You're driving. Mpho you'll watch Robert."

"Okay," Mpho nodded.

"Mpho."

"Yeah?"

"Get my vest out of the car for me please." She threw her car keys to Mpho.

"Sure."

Nolwazi took the audio bag, Mpho grabbed the tripod with the mounted camera, and they left the room.

"Robert."

"Yes."

"Listen to me carefully."

"I'm listening. Carefully."

"You will be live internationally."

"Still think it's a bad idea."

"So please be very careful of what you say. People will be listening to you and some of them may feel uncomfortable with what you have to say. So please, no bombshells."

"Don't drop bombs, got it."

"Let's go." Mandisa grabbed her laptop and led Robert out to the Union Bay Newsroom Live van.

The sirens got louder as the police vehicles became more visible. A white car was far ahead of them. She knew it was Thabiso.

"That's not good, you have to go."

"There's a secret gate around back, that we can use."

"Where's Nolwazi?"

"She said she had to go back for the transmitter."

"And my vest?"

"She has it with her, asked her to grab it while I was setting up, which reminds me, you'll have to watch the camera and try to hold the tripod steady while we're on the road."

"I'm not going."

"Right, sorry, uhm, that means I'll have to do it because Nolwazi's driving."

"For now, drive around to the back, we'll meet you there."

"Mandisa—"

"Go!"

"Don't have to tell me twice." Robert jumped into the back and closed the door.

With a groan, Mpho jumped into the driver's seat and turned the key in the ignition as Mandisa ran back into the house.

"Nolwazi?" She ran into the living room, where she found the anchor grabbing a cable and a device that she guessed to be the transmitter. "You have to go."

"Okay, could you just grab that box over there," she pointed to a box closer to Mandisa.

Tyres screeched outside as Mandisa picked the box up. "You're out of time. Go through the back."

Nolwazi ran to the kitchen and burst through the door, Mandisa hot on her tail.

"Come on, come on, come on," Mpho repeated.

Robert opened the door and Nolwazi jumped in, grabbing the box from the detective and setting it aside the tripod. As Mandisa was closing the door, Nolwazi stopped her. "I dropped the battery," she jumped out before Mandisa could respond and ran back into the house.

"Come on."

"Xaba!" a voice yelled from the shadows of the house. "When will you stop running?"

"I'm not running." She raised her hands in surrender.

"Good. Because all the evidence points to you. You're only fooling yourself."

"Well, I guess she's fooling me too," Mpho jumped out through the passenger's seat and stepped in front of Mandisa.

"Now's not the time to play hero Seme. You were good playing for our side."

"That's where you're wrong. I never was 'playing' for you," he glanced down at his watch. "I was stalling. Just like I am now."

Mandisa's computer beeped. With a glance over her shoulder, she could see on the screen that it had a location. "It's done."

"What's done?"

"We have the location of Mandla."

"Tell me you're joking."

"I can't. Someone has to bring the truth out and it seems like you and your buddies don't care much to do that."

"Mandisa, don't make me shoot."

"Thabiso I can do a lot of things. But I can't make you pull that trigger."

"Mandisa."

"I know the truth now. And soon everyone will. But if you pull that trigger, it all comes to nothing."

Creeping from behind Thabiso, the news anchor knocked him on the side of the head with a rock. The detective fell with a thud.

"Let's go." Nolwazi ran to the van.

Mpho jumped into the driver's seat and Nolwazi threw the battery at Mandisa. The detective caught it just as Nolwazi pushed her into the van.

"What are you doing?"

The door slammed shut. Mandisa got up to look at Nolwazi on the other side of the glass. "What are you doing?"

"I'm sorry, but they need you," Nolwazi explained from the outside.

Mandisa struggled against the door. "Nolwazi, open the door." She repeatedly pulled the handle of the door.

Nolwazi threw on Mandisa's bulletproof vest, zipped it up and took a step back. Carefully, she pulled her weave off and tucked it into the vest.

Mpho turned the key in the ignition.

"Nolwazi, you have no idea what you're doing. You're gonna get yourself killed."

"Just another Friday," the anchor replied as she combed her natural hair into an afro as similar as possible to Mandisa's style with the braids on the front half. "Go."

Mpho released the handbrake and the car sped off, crashing through the back wooden gate and down the street.

"No!" Mandisa banged against the window. As they lost visual of the house, a gunshot echoed into the atmosphere.

CHAPTER 36

IT WAS QUIET IN THE car for a while. The clock on the radio read **19:49** as Mpho followed the directions of the GPS to the location Mandisa had found.

Once she had rendered what happened, the detective looked at Mpho. "You knew she would do that?"

"I'm sorry."

"You're sorry? You just put a civilian life at risk and all you have to say for it is I'm sorry?"

"She knows what she's doing."

"Did you not hear that gunshot? She's a defenceless journalist against armed police officers, how do you think that will end."

"What do you expect from me Mandisa? Do you want me to turn back? Want me to say I regret leaving her behind, well I do. But she's the only one who actually chose to look at the facts. Too many people have been killed. How many more would be killed before Mandla faces justice? He needs to be caught."

"At what cost?"

Mpho opened his mouth, but no words came out. His grip tightened on the steering wheel. "She chose this."

"That wasn't her call to make."

"What's done is done. Like you said, I've been backing your play this whole time, now it's your turn to back mine."

"Yeah, remind me never to give you that choice again."

"Tense."

"Would it kill you to not speak for five minutes?"

Robert shrunk into his seat at the remark.

The silence echoed once again.

NOLWAZI REMAINED IN place, on her knees and head bowed as uniformed officers surrounded her. She kept her hands raised above her head.

Captain Sithole approached her. "Mandisa Xaba, you are under arrest for suspicion of the murder of Nozizwe Biyela." He lowered Nolwazi's arms, pulled out his handcuffs and locked them on the woman's wrists. "Why did you do it?" He pulled her up.

"Sir," Thabiso shook off the shock, his eyes focusing on the woman's clothes. "That's not Mandisa."

"She's on her way to the real killer." Nolwazi turned to face the captain. "You might want to tune into Union Bay Newsroom Live before the confession ends."

"What confession?"

"Robert Zietsman's confession."

Sithole groaned, "You have no idea the trouble you're in. Who has the app?"

"You can use my phone," Nolwazi offered. "But you'll have to uncuff me. Unless I'm under arrest."

"I suggest you choose your friends more wisely," he uncuffed Nolwazi. "You could've been killed."

It was then the news anchor realized whoever had taken the shot missed or wasn't aiming for her. But whoever it was would've been hard to pinpoint now. "Death is the price of justice," Nolwazi replied as she pulled out her phone and swiped on the screen. She was already logged onto the UBNL App. She clicked on the Livestream and a mid-shot of a presenter filled the screen. Nolwazi handed the phone to Sithole.

"...JOINED BY INVESTOR and author of *Into the Money Mind: The Millionaire Mindset*, Robert Zietsman," the presenter explained from the studio. "Robert, thank you so much for your time."

"I... Thank you." The camera was a bit shaky. You could hear the Tyres on the asphalt in the background.

"Now, it's to my understanding that you would like to address something about the man who has been dubbed the Premeditator. What information do you have exactly, and how did you come about it?"

"The Premeditator," he sighed. "Mandla Magwaza..." he looked away from the camera. A voice spoke from behind the camera forcing him to refocus. "Mandla used to work for me. He, uhm... he was one of our best. Young and eager to learn." He inhaled then exhaled heavily. "One day, he discovered some information that... he wasn't supposed to know. That made some... people... unhappy. Some very powerful people."

"Can you tell us who those people are?"

"I can't. And even if I knew, I wouldn't. It wouldn't be wise to cross them."

"What did he do with said information?"

"He threatened to take it to the authorities, the police, the media. He poked a sleeping beast... and the beast fought back."

"When you say beast, you're referring to the people you said you can't mention?"

"Yes."

"And what information exactly is it that he found?"

"Information about..." he looked away again, struggling to speak. He shook his head, "about the Founding Five."

"Do you know who the five are?"

"Only Zenzele Msani knew for sure. 'No identities' was the agreement. But after he died... that all changed. Now the other three are dead too."

"So, you were one of them?"

Robert groaned. "I am," he replied through gritted teeth. "The last one standing," he mumbled.

"And what information is it that Mr Magwaza found?"

Robert looked away again, and the soft voice behind the camera returned. "That Union Bay," he looked into the camera, "was built through corrupt contracts, blackmail, and..." he bowed his head. "And life-ending threats."

"Is that the same information that Lihle Maphumulo in court said Mandla took to the media?"

"I suppose."

"Mr Zietsman, I can't imagine how difficult this has to be for you, so I have to ask... the statements you've just made, are you under any compulsion?"

No reply.

"Mr Zietsman?"

"No. I'm speaking from a place of liberality and clear-mindedness. I know exactly what I'm saying. This secret has been eating away at me for a long time so I'm glad the truth is out in the open now."

"Thank you so much for your time, Mr Zietsman. I'm sure, the authorities, wherever they are working tirelessly to solve this case."

ONLY AFTER ENDING THE transmission and switching off the camera did Mandisa realize that the van had stopped.

"We're here," Mpho mumbled.

Mandisa glanced at the radio. 20:01.

CHAPTER 37

THE OLD BUILDING WAS burnt through, but the foundation was strong. The ground floor was the most easily accessible, and the most vulnerable, yet it was the safest.

Mandisa stepped out of the vehicle and instructed Mpho and Robert to stay inside.

"What do you think she's doing?"

"It's Mandisa, who knows what's happening in that woman's head." He looked out the window, only catching sight of the detective's left side, Mpho noticed that she was holding something to her ear. Her head was doing a good job concealing it, but Mpho guessed it to be a phone. After a few moments, Mpho tried to look away as the detective turned on her heel and made her way back to the van.

Mandisa opened the door for Robert. "Let's go."

"You don't think it's a bad idea to bring him with us?"

"It wouldn't be wise to leave him here."

"I won't go anywhere."

"Forgive me if I don't believe. Now get out."

As Mpho and Robert pilled out of the van, Mandisa drew her gun, checked the magazine, then exhaled heavily, four bullets, no stare magazine. She slide it back in place and cocked the gun.

"That's just in case, right?" said Robert.

Mandisa gave him a look that told him she wouldn't answer the question. "Let's go."

Mpho and Robert shared a hesitant look but followed Mandisa into the building, or what was left of it.

A BEEP FROM THE 28-inch screen drew Mandla's attention. "No," he protested as he watched Mandisa, Mpho and Robert walk into the building. He rushed to a table fully decked with chemicals, glass tubes and used syringes.

AS THEY WORKED THEIR way through the rubble of the building, the sound of glasses pressing against each other came from the floor above them.

"Stay behind me, and try to stay hidden." Mandisa pulled out her phone, switched the torch on then reduced its intensity to the lowest it could go. She held the device right-side up in her left hand and slung it below her outstretched gun-holding right hand. She took quick steps towards the source of the noise, shining her phone to the ground after every few steps then lifting it forward again. Moving sideways up the stairs, she was careful not to step on anything that might give away her position. At the top of the stairs, she turned quickly and leaned against the wall, quickly looking into the large room before she ducked back to safety. Mandisa saw equipment that was neatly placed on tables around the room, but she couldn't see Mandla anywhere. She flinched at the sound of a rock skidding across the floor on the lower level.

Looking up to the corner Mandisa tucked herself in, Mpho mouthed, "Sorry."

"You're becoming a nuisance, detective."

"You're terrorising my city."

"Your city? I disagree. What do you think Mr Seme? You think she's a KUB City baby?"

Mandisa took a deep breath and closed her eyes while releasing it. "You're stalling which means you don't have a plan to escape. You've got nowhere to run."

"And here I was thinking you're doing the same thing."

"Let's make a deal. You come out now and I'll convince the judge to go easy on you."

"Tempting, but we both know you don't have that kind of power detective. But you know who does?"

"Enlighten me." She leaned to check the room again and as she ducked away, a bullet hit the wall next to her. Her breathing picked up speed.

"Close call detective. You're quite the daredevil, I give you that."

The memory of Tuesday night tugged at the detective. She shook it off. The burning sensation returned to her stomach. She tried to ignore it. No one was going to get hurt today, she couldn't allow it, she wouldn't.

"I'd say that's noble," Mandla continued. "But it's stupid." Three bullets shattered the wall, barely missing the detective's arm as the concrete fragments flew.

"Guess that's where you're wrong," her voice an interval deeper as she switched the phone torch off. "I'm far from noble." She slowly lowered herself to the ground as she checked the bullets in the magazine then slide it back in place and cocked the gun. Tilting her head slightly, she could see Mandla standing behind one of the tables with his gun aiming somewhere above her head. He didn't realize she had switched her vantage point, so she took the opportunity, aimed and fired at Mandla's shoulder. She heard him groan as he went down with a thud.

The detective got to her feet and rushed into the room. "Mandla Magwaza. You're under arrest for the murder of Nduduzo and Nozizwe Biyela," she pocketed her phone.

"Nice trick."

"Consider yourself lucky that I didn't kill you, even though you gave me the grounds to."

"And that's what we call police brutality. But this is not how it was supposed to end," he removed his hand from his wounded shoulder, revealing a flash grenade as he tossed it into the air and rolled away from the detective.

As she ducked away, the grenade went off, the impact sending her to the ground. She felt her head buzzing as her vision blurred.

Mandisa shook her head, trying to fight through the pain. She tried to look around, her eyes still burning a bit as she realized she had blacked out for long enough for her other half to escalate the situation. Her plan had gone to waste. All she knew was that if she couldn't see, she'd have to hear. "You wanted me to solve your riddles, and I did," she said softly. "You wanted Robert's confession to be broadcasted and it was. So why don't you tell me exactly what it is you really want."

"You... You detective were supposed to arrest Zietsman. Not me."

"You killed three people."

"Call it justice!"

The detective focused on Mandla's voice, trying to locate him. She knew she had to provoke him a little more, but without giving away where she was. "I wouldn't call revenge justice. Not now and not ever."

"She says it like it is," Mpho yelled from afar.

Mandla scoffed. "I'm intrigued detective. You caught me by surprise and that doesn't happen often. So, tell me, how were you able to pull it off?"

She could hear Mandla's voice towards her right. "Does it matter?"

"I suppose it doesn't all that much, but I mean come on, what would it hurt?"

Mandisa sighed, her eyes beginning to adjust to the darkness. She couldn't yet see fully but she knew that she had to draw Mandla out more. "When you requested to talk to Mpho, I knew you'd be watching him."

"So, you made him go to the police while you went on the run?"

"Actually, I volunteered," the journalist corrected.

"Mpho."

"Yeah?"

"Stop talking."

Mandla chuckled. "Because if you weren't working with the police, that would make me believe that you were working with me."

"You might just be as smart as you make yourself seem."

"So, you staged the call, but you couldn't have anticipated that I wanted to get caught."

"No. I don't think anyone saw that coming. After that stunt you pulled in court, creating reasonable doubt, shifting the blame to me, and conveniently disappearing, it became obvious that you could work with anyone you wanted to because you had the resources to blackmail them."

"And the banker?"

"That thing he used to kill himself, you gave it to him, didn't you?"

"What does it matter?" There was a light shuffle of feet after the question.

"I suppose it doesn't, but what would it hurt?"

Mandisa could almost hear a smile tug on Mandla's lips. "Nice try detective. So, when the two of you argued about the journalist wanting to go to the police..."

"It was an act," Mandisa added. "We knew you were listening."

"My, my, my, and here I was thinking that I'm the conductor, but it turns out you were."

"Good."

Mandla could feel the cold muzzle of a gun on the back of his neck.

"Now let's try this again. You're under arrest for the murder of Nduduzo and Nozizwe Biyela."

Mandla lifted his hands in surrender. "Colour me impressed."

"What about Vihaan?" Robert whispered to the journalist.

"There's no proof to convict him for that. And also, Vihaan's death would be considered a suicide rather than a homicide, unless Mandla admits he provided the chemical that killed Vihaan."

"Anything you say or do can and will be used against you in the court of law. You have the right to—"

"I know my rights detective." With a sigh, he smoothed down his clothes as he got up.

"Regardless, it's part of my job to—"

"Recite them to me?" Mandla interrupted. "Oh, believe me, I know that all too well," he lowered his arms and held them behind his back. "That must be exhausting."

Cautiously, Mandisa replaced her gun in its holster and pulled out her handcuffs. "You have the right to an attorney, if you cannot afford one, one will be provided for you," she ended locking the cuffs around Mandla's wrists. Her vision had returned just in time for her to see Mpho and Robert as they approached.

"I'm curious. How did you expect to kill me while you're sitting here?"

"Patience Mr Zietsman." He turned around to face Mandisa, Mpho and Robert. "Every story has a conclusion, and every good conclusion consists of two key elements. A surprising yet inevitable ending."

"What does that mean?"

"It means... I wasn't."

"Wasn't what?"

"I wasn't going to kill you, you fool. You see, for you Mr Zietsman, death would have been the easy way out. So, look at what is happening to your beloved kingdom you worked so hard to build," he indicated to a computer with a nod of his head.

They all turned to a screen displaying the shares of RZ Investments as they came crashing.

"No."

"You brought this upon yourself, Robert."

"No, no, no, no," he turned and rushed at Mandla.

The detective pressed her hand on Robert's chest. "Don't."

"So you wanted to get caught, again?" Mpho's brow furrowed. "That doesn't make any sense."

"This is KwaZulu Union Bay, there are very few things that make any sense in this city. However, if I'm being honest, I didn't account to 'get caught,' but I have accepted my fate. There is no stopping what's to come."

"What's to come?" the journalist asked.

"Alas. For now, order must be restored. Faith must be brought back into this broken system of ours because people need something to believe in. Someone," he focused on Mandisa, "to believe in. But you know, it's funny how happiness and success tear people apart, yet tragedy is what brings them together."

At Mandla's revelation, the detective couldn't ignore the thought of her aunt's invitation to visit her mother's grave.

"It is unfortunate that we are no acceptation of this sad truth."

"What are you talking about?" said Mpho.

"A rogue detective, an investigative journalist, a man with many secrets and a man who wants to shine some light in the dark. Again. It's unfortunate that it took tragedies to bring the four of us together." He closed his eyes. "Can you hear it? Like sheep to their shepherd," he opened his eyes to look at Mandisa. "Here they come."

From a distance, sirens rang. Barely audible at first but they got louder with each second.

"This is the beauty of life. It's unpredictable nature. It keeps our purpose in check."

"You're crazy, you know that?" Robert tried to take a step closer even against the force of Mandisa's hand still on his chest. "You're a madman and I did the city, in fact, I did the world a favour by putting you behind bars."

"Be careful Robert." Mandisa finally shoved Robert away from Mandla.

"And you know what?" he stared Mandla in the eye. "I don't regret any of it. So, if I was given the choice and the opportunity, I would do it again. Over and over and over again."

"Okay, that's it. I didn't want to do this here, but you've left me no choice." Mandisa pulled out another set of handcuffs. "Robert Zietsman, you're under arrest for fraud, money laundering and fabricating evidence."

"Wait," he held his hands out to try and keep Mandisa away. "I can explain."

"Yeah, I'm sure the judge can't wait to hear what you have to say. I on the other hand don't care." She marched towards Robert as he backed away. "Anything you say or do can and will be used against you in the court of law."

"Wait, I'm sure there's something we can work out."

Mandla shook his head.

"Are you even listening to me?" Mandisa stepped closer.

Robert opened his mouth, but no response came out.

"You're already looking at twenty-five years at the least, and yet you want to add bribery to your list of offences."

"No, wait, wait, I take it back." Robert clapped his hands together, "Please, think about this."

"I have." Seeing the opportunity, Mandisa clicked the handcuffs around Robert's wrists.

"You're making a mistake."

"So I've been told throughout my career. Fortunately for me, my mistakes seem to get things done."

"You'll regret this."

"Is that a threat?"

"Sounds like a threat to me," Mandla suggested.

"You're not helping."

"And what makes you think I'd help you; you deluded catalyst of white-collar crime?"

Mpho let out a low whistle.

"Get up," Mandisa instructed.

Without a word, Mandla obeyed the order, using his hands to get on a knee and then to his feet.

Mandisa pulled her gun out, aiming at Mandla. "Both of you, move, now," she nudged her head towards the exit.

Mandla led the way, but Robert merely glared at the detective, not moving a muscle.

"You want me to repeat myself?" The muzzle of the gun shifted its attention to Robert.

"Okay, okay, I'm moving."

With Mandla leading the way out, Robert followed and Mandisa watched them from behind, Mpho following close behind. It was a quiet walk out of the building and Mandisa couldn't help smiling a little, glad that it was all over. Her mind started drifting to the thought of being home and finally having time to relax for the first time this week. As they got closer to the exit, the flashing blue lights got brighter.

"You can still reconsider this."

Mandla suddenly stopped, causing Robert to bump into him. "You still don't get it?" he shook his head. He turned to face Robert. "She's not one of those skew cops you can just tip off ngezibandayo or with a few hundred. She has a hero essence about her."

"I don't know what that means."

"It means unlike me; she's actually holding out hope to you. Because for some crazy reason, she must think that sick people like you are worth saving. And you should be very grateful for that because if it were up to me, people like you... the whole lot of you would be—"

"That's enough," the detective stepped in. "Keep walking. I don't like repeating myself."

Mandla took a step back. "I would highly advise you to be careful with this one detective. Be very careful because as soon as you turn your back to him, he won't hesitate to rip out your spine. And I think today proved that." He turned on his heel and walked out of the building.

Swallowing almost audibly, Robert glanced ever so slightly over his shoulder. The detective and the journalist both had their eyes on him as if heeding Mandla's warning. With a sigh, Robert squared his shoulders and walked out, Mpho and Mandisa followed after him.

The police officers were standing with their guns drawn, using the open doors of their vehicles as shields. Mpho's arms instinctively shot up.

"Put your hands down."

"Don't you see the guns pointing at us? When someone pulls out a gun, your hands go up."

"I'm a detective."

"And they think you killed someone."

"What did I say about repeating myself?"

Mpho finally lowered his arms.

"Well, I'll be. She did it," Thabiso moved away from his hiding place. "Stand down," he yelled.

The officers all straightened up and lowered their weapons while keeping their focus on Mandisa's group.

Thabiso approached them. "Mandisa Xaba,"

"Simelane."

"You're under arrest for the murder of Vihaan Naicker."

"You can't be serious."

"Do I look like I'm joking?" He pulled his handcuffs out and moved behind Mandisa, who held her hands behind her back without further objection.

"You don't look like you know what a joke is," Mandla responded.

"Anything you say or do," he locked one side of the cuffs, "can and will be used against you in the court of law," he locked the other side.

"You have no grounds to arrest her."

"Yeah, like you'd know."

"Actually, I would, because what killed Vihaan was concentrated rat poisoning which I highly doubt she could mix herself, with all due respect detective."

"Rat poisoning," Thabiso scoffed.

Mandisa brought her hands out from behind her, dangling the locked handcuffs in hand.

"Oh, oh," Mandla chuckled.

"Thank you for that confession. It just made things easier for us. Because trying to find a way to exonerate this know-it-all," he indicated to Mandisa, "would've taken longer than her patience would allow her."

Mandisa gave the handcuffs back to Thabiso.

"How'd you know that would work?" asked Thabiso.

"I didn't."

"Yet you sounded so sure on the call."

"Lovely," Captain Sithole approached. "Now that we have that out of the way, can someone tell me why Robert Zietsman is in handcuffs?"

"With all due respect Captain, it would be a great insult to have to answer that after the events of today."

"Both of you, with me," his jaw clenched as he walked out of earshot.

Sharing a defeated look, Mandisa and Thabiso walked over to the captain.

"That man," he pointed in the direction of Robert. "Is worth just about three of your lifetimes. He outmonies us, outranks us and therefore outpowers us."

Mandisa considered mentioning that due to the tanking of his company's stock price, he no longer outmonies them thereby rendering the captain's statement void. Instead, she said, "Just because things are the way they are doesn't mean they have to stay that way."

Thabiso opened his mouth, then closed it again. "Sir... this is probably the first time, and possibly the last time, but I'm with Xaba on this. The law is the law. If we start making exceptions in it for certain individuals," he glanced over his shoulder, "we might as well be reversing all the way back to the Apartheid era."

The captain couldn't ignore their arguments. But he also couldn't go against the person who he was receiving orders from. He weighed the options.

A silent thud was followed by the falling of a body. The captain and the detectives quickly turned and saw the body on the ground.

Robert Zietsman.

"No!" Mandisa drew her gun, her eyes sweeping across the crowd of policemen and women as she approached Robert.

The officers all drew their guns, cautiously ducking.

"Who took that shot?" the captain yelled. "Who took that shot?"

Mandisa looked down at the body. Then she returned her attention to the ocean of officers.

"Is he okay?" Thabiso approached.

"Shot to the chest. He's dead."

"Sniper," Mandla added. "Possibly close range."

"Did you do this?"

"How could I have possibly done this?" Mandla revealed his handcuffed hands from behind his back.

Mandisa thought back to Mandla's earlier words, 'and every good conclusion consists of two key elements. A surprising yet inevitable ending.' She looked at Mandla but remained silent.

"Did you do it?"

"Captain, stop," Thabiso intervened. "Mandisa, you think it could be him?"

Without shifting her attention away from Mandla, the detective replied, "No. At this point he's just as along for the ride as the rest of us. It goes back to something Robert told me earlier..." she looked at the body on the ground. "There are some people at play that we don't know about. The true governors of this city's politics."

"Everyone is going back to the station in a convoy led by me. In your cars, now!" Sithole yelled. "Mandisa you'll be following from the back of the convoy."

Mandisa nodded.

"Thabiso—"

"Babysitting," he interrupted. "I know."

With a nod, the captain grabbed Mandla and hauled him to his car. Around him, the officers climbed into their vehicles. Mandisa and Mpho got into the van that they arrived in. It somehow felt empty. Then Nolwazi popped up in front of the van. Mandisa felt a soothing relief wash over her, her lips tugging at the corners.

Sithole opened the back door of his car and Mandla stepped in. "Oh, how the plot thickens," said Mandla looking at the activities around him as the captain moved around the car to the driver's seat. "Enter the epilogue."

CHAPTER 38

KwaZulu Union Bay City, November 4th, 2023

IN FRONT OF THE CITY hall, a large crowd of civilians gathered, looking at the mayor standing on the podium. On his left stood police captain, Sithole and on the right of the mayor was Detective Xaba and Mpho Seme.

Mayor Phumelela Sithole looked at his notes and then lifted his head to face the crowd. A woman in a black SUV with the window rolled down caught his eyes. He thought he recognised her, but he couldn't put a name to the face. "My fellow citizens of KwaZulu Union Bay City. On this day, seventeen years and a day ago, one of my great predecessors stood at this very podium and welcomed many of you to this land of new opportunities. Over the past three days, our city has faced a terrorist threat, which has been dealt with thanks to our brave police force led by Captain Sithole," he indicated to his left. "Who worked very closely on this with Detective Xaba and investigative journalist from Union Bay City News, Mpho Seme," he indicated to his right. "A round of applause for their courage and selflessness in the line of danger."

Subduing a grunt, Mpho looked at the detective in the corner of his eye. She looked well-composed as the crowd clapped and shouted in celebration of them.

The mayor took a deep breath. "However, it is unfortunate and with a heavy heart that I stand here today to tell you that our city was founded upon the corruption and lies of well-dressed criminals."

Mandisa's eyes drifted to a man and woman making their way out of the crowd. The woman looked back, making eye contact with the detective. "Thando," she muttered.

"Men and women who would do anything to get their will," the mayor continued. "It is our sad reality that we had to find out about such atrocities through the deaths of..." He took a moment to himself. "Through unfortunate and unnecessary deaths which left blood streaming down our streets. These secrets which were held in the name of our city will not be condoned and such secrets will be brought into the light. Working with the KwaZulu Union Police Services, my office will be launching an investigation into the so-called Founding Five. We will find whatever else has been hidden under the foundations of our city and we will hold all those who are responsible accountable. And to all those who are part of the violence and gang wars that have broken out throughout the city, we will find you, and you will face the full force of the law, without possibility of pardon. Crime will not be tolerated, and corruption will be eradicated. This is my promise to you!"

Thando and the man she was with had disappeared from the crowd. The woman in the SUV rolled her window up as the vehicle pulled out of the parking bay and drove down the street. The number plate reading **NTETHA 7 – KUB.**

CHAPTER 39

THE COURTROOM WAS NOT as packed and noisy as it was yesterday. A lot of calls had to be made and a lot of meetings were had to make Mandla's trial happen on a Saturday. Therefore, the judge wanted to keep it short and simple.

"Mandla Magwaza. You are charged with the murder of Vihaan Naicker, Nduduzo Biyela and Nozizwe Biyela. How do you plead?"

"Guilty."

The small gallery exploded in applause and shouts of celebration. The judge banged his gavel, calling for order. "Mr Magwaza, excluding Mr Naicker's murder, you were previously charged for these same murders by the Honourable Judge Nonkululeko Msimang, and you pleaded not guilty. Therefore, by your testimony today, I am also charging you with perjury."

Mandisa got up and walked out as the judge explained the details of Mandla's conviction. She knew he'd be going away for a much longer time than he was previously gone for and to a far more dangerous prison, one that was certainly outside of Union Bay. She stood at the entrance of the building and looked upon the horizon. The view of the city was beautiful from there, even in the middle of the day. Captain Sithole joined her.

"I believe I owe you an apology."

"Well, you don't."

"Let me finish. I doubted you, sent the whole department after you and painted you as a killer. I was wrong about you."

"You were. But you also misled everyone into thinking Nozizwe was killed over the weekend which bought me the time I needed to look into her murder."

"I'm glad you got the message."

"What you thought at the beginning of the case doesn't matter now. What matters is what you believe now."

Sithole nodded. "You'll make a great captain one day."

"Actually, I don't think I will." Mandisa pulled her Baretta m9 and her badge out and held them to the captain.

"What are you doing?"

"Consider this my official letter of resignation."

"I can't accept this."

"You'll have to."

"This city is falling apart right now because of this power vacuum between crime bosses. I need you; this city needs you, now more than ever."

Mandisa thought back to Mandla's words about the city needing someone to believe in. "Unfortunately, that's too bad, and a little too late. I made a promise at the beginning of this Premeditator case, and I fully intend to keep it. It's time for me to leave the badge behind and move on."

"Mandisa," the captain tried to plead.

"My written and signed letter is already on your table back at the station." She squared her shoulders a final time before the captain. "It may not have always been pleasant, but it was an honour working with you, Jobe."

"Nonkosi," with a sigh, Sithole accepted the gun and badge. "Are you sure this is what you want?"

"Maybe not what I want, but it is what I need." With that, she walked down the stairs and stepped into her car. She grabbed her diary from the passenger's seat and opened it to a page folded to mark the last used page. Grabbing her pen from the compartment on her door, she wrote.

Thank you for your help through this case, I couldn't have done it without you. But no one can ever know about this.

She signed her name and then flipped to the page where her other persona listed the conditions.

1. You have to disobey Sithole's orders. He won't trust you, so you can't trust anyone. Except me, or should I say yourself.
2. Once the case is done, resign your badge as detective.

The first condition had a tick next to it. Mandisa ticked the second condition then shut the book, writing on the front cover:

THE PREMEDITATOR
CASE 1

CHAPTER 40

UNION BAY CITY NEWS was always heavily busy at the end of the year, but today even more so following the closing of the biggest case in years. It was actually "the biggest case the city has ever had" according to the new article Mpho Seme was working on. He wasn't wrong, corruption, fraud, blackmail, murder, and almost every type of crime was revealed and/or committed over the past three days.

"It was detective turned accused killer who actually cracked the case wide open. Her ability to solve riddles and tirelessly track leads is the reason Mandla Magwaza was finally arrested with solid evidence. Having solved the case, she also found evidence that would've put Nduduzo Biyela, otherwise known as Mkhonto or the Kingpin, away for decades. All those who worked for him are already being tracked down and arrested by the authorities. To the brave detective, we greatly owe much gratitude to you." Mpho looked over the article and clicked the publish button with great satisfaction.

"I have a lot of faith in you Mpho," Sizwe began. "But I'm not sure even your article could stop the hell and havoc happening outside. And where is your detective now?"

"I think she's done enough, and we can leave her alone."

"Okay, fair point, but the people are angry, and they want someone to blame. So, I'd be very surprised if the mayor was still in office come Monday morning."

"I thought you said you have 'a lot of faith' in him." Jess leaned on the wall of Mpho's cubicle with a smile and a sparkle in her eye.

Sizwe looked between them before taking a step back and ducking away.

"How are you feeling?"

"Like you owe me lunch for saving your life."

"I'm glad you're better." He glanced around the office floor before turning to Jess again. "How about you come over for dinner tonight? And the day after, and the day after that."

Jess tilted her head, the corner of her lips twitching.

"It'll take me a while to adjust to Hayley not being around."

"Did you just ask me to move in?"

"Well, considering what happened here two days ago, I think it's safer to stick together, you know."

Jess stepped forward, cupped Mpho's chin and planted her lips on his. Time seemed to stop for a few sweet and tender moments before Jess pulled away. "I hope that answers your question."

CHAPTER 41

WAVES OF EMOTIONS WASHED over the former detective as she stepped out of her car and onto the graveyard grounds. Her family was already waiting for her, all dressed in white garments.

"I'm so glad you came," her aunt embraced her. "I'm sorry," she whispered. "I'm sorry I thought—"

"It's okay. It's all in the past," she took a step back.

Together with the rest of the family, they walked to the small patch of land where Nontle was laid to rest several years ago. "We'll give you a little space but we're right here, okay?" Zintle rubbed her niece's back.

"Okay."

Her aunt led the family a few feet away as Mandisa looked at her mother's name engraved on the granite. She bent her knees so she may be at eye level with the engraving.

Mandisa never really believed that speaking to a tombstone allowed the person to hear you, but her family always said it helped. It was only at that moment when she laid eyes on her mother's tombstone for the first time that she realized what they meant by that. It was a small tugging feeling called closure. And that's when she knew that since her mother died, it was not closure she wanted. It was revenge.

"Ma," Mandisa began. "I've missed you. You were always there for me, always loving me, protecting me... right till the end," she sighed. "I wouldn't be who I am today if it weren't for... if it weren't for you." She wiped the tear straying from her eye and took a moment to compose herself. "I promise you that I will find the people who put you here, and there will be justice. I promise..."

As Mandisa got back up, her family joined her, warmly embracing her.

Mandisa's eyes never left her mother's name. "Whatever it takes," she whispered.

DUMO XABA

Acknowledgements

I WOULD LIKE TO EXPRESS my heartfelt gratitude to my team who supported me behind the scenes, the Dumo Xaba Studios team, and my test readers.

BASIPHILE NKOMONDE: I extend my heartfelt gratitude to her for her unwavering support and patience in navigating the intricacies of the Xhosa language.

MANTOA HLOPHE: A SPECIAL acknowledgement for the dedicated efforts in reviewing and providing valuable feedback that contributed to the coherence of this novel. Her commitment to the finer details ensured simplicity and clarity.

MENZI MYENI: TO WHOM I am deeply thankful for his keen insights, thoughtful cliques and constructive feedback which played a pivotal role in refining the narrative.

I EXTEND MY PROFOUND appreciation to an unnamed police officer whose invaluable insights and expertise in law enforcement greatly enriched the authenticity of this novel.

WHO IS MANDISA XABA?

PERSONAL LIFE

Mandisa Xaba was born and raised in Durban, KwaZulu-Natal before the family moved to KwaZulu Union Bay City. After the unfortunate passing of her mother, Mandisa wanted to become a police officer, pledging to make it her life's work to clean the streets of KwaZulu Union Bay City.

After moving out from home to attend university, she tried to stay as far away from her family as much as possible, even though her aunt, Zintle is constantly reaching out to her.

HOBBIES

Mandisa enjoys binge-watching law series with a glass of wine. Annually, she reads one personal development book and two fiction novels (one South African and one International).

WORK

After graduating from criminology, she began her career working as a policewoman, where she worked for four years to become a detective, a role she has been in for the past three years. Many times, she did not get along with her captain due to her over-ambition, rogue methods and chasing after dangerous cases without consultation.

EPILOGUE

KwaZulu Union Bay City, March 4th, 2024

AFTER RESIGNING, IT took the former detective months to find Steven de Villiers, the man her mother got shot trying to help. She thought it impossible to convince him to help her given how fearful he still was of the organisation he used to work for. Having been in protective custody for well over a decade, it seemed as though he really wasn't going to risk his life helping Mandisa, until she pulled the "My mother died trying to save you" card. She vividly remembered the life draining from Steven's face when she said that. Mandisa shook off the memory. She couldn't let the past steal any more time from her, she was finally going to get information that could help her investigation into her mother's death and the real reason behind the war between the city's two biggest crime families which has been fought in the shadows for as long as Mandisa could recall.

"Usuphelile u-petrol wakho," said her driver as the car pulled to a stop.

She thanked him and handed him three hundred Rand notes. The driver offered her a fifty Rand note but she dismissed it, "Keep it, it's your tip." The man made no argument as Mandisa stepped out of the vehicle. After a moment, the car continued its drive down the road. Mandisa waited till it turned the corner then she made her way up the road, walking past a few houses they had driven past. She crossed the street and took a left turn. It took her a few minutes to get to Steven's house. Once she did, she knocked on the door and waited. After a short while, she knocked again. Again, no response. Feeling uneasy, Mandisa walked around to the back of the house, pulled two hair clips out of her hair, and got to work on the door. She closed her eyes, listening carefully, until she heard the click. While taking a few glances around the backyard, she wiped her hairpins on a small black cloth before replacing them in her hair. She slipped on a pair of black gloves, and a black balaclava attached to the hood of her hoodie, concealing everything but her eyes before she opened the door. Mandisa quickly searched the dining room, the living room, and then the bathroom. Pulling her unregistered firearm out, she opened the door to the main bedroom and stepped inside. Seeing the body lying in a pool of blood, memories from the day she met Steven came flooding back, the fear she felt, the bullets flying, her mother's body in her hands, and her final words.

"You have to go Mandisa, it's not safe... Ngiyakuthanda..."

Mandisa wrestled the memories back into the mental cage she had imprisoned them as she tucked her gun back in place. She pulled out her phone and took a few pictures and a video of the room. What Steven was worried about had happened, he was found and eliminated. This was the big risk of helping Mandisa with the investigation, and he had warned her. But she couldn't think about that at the moment, only where Steven hid the evidence. Where he thought would be the best place to hide something he didn't want to be found by his former employees but seen by Mandisa. She opened the first drawer of his chest of drawers and searched for anything that she thought was out of place. She closed it and opened the next one. She moved the neatly folded shirts around and at the back of the drawer, she found a toy gun. During their last interactions, Steven had revealed his pledge not to use guns anymore, but what could he be using a toy for? As she moved to put it back, she felt something moved in it. She shook it and heard the movement. She cracked the toy in half and a USB fell out. Tossing the two halves of the toy aside, she picked up the USB.

"Hands up," said a voice behind Mandisa. "Now."

Slowly Mandisa bowed her head and shoved the USB through the gap in her hoodie into the back of her afro before she lifted her hands and her head.

"Now turn around."

She followed the instructions. "Detective Thabiso Simelane."

"You know me?"

"Very well."

"I can say the same about you. You have no idea how long I've been waiting for this. I'm tired of you people who think you can do as you please and expect the police to turn a blind eye. Vigilantism has always been and will always be a crime."

"You're not exactly using the usual police protocol, detective."

"Let's just say I had a bad influence as a colleague."

"Had. What happened?"

"She moved on."

"Right. So do you want me to apologize now or later?"

"For what?"

"Stealing your car."

"Nice try," Thabiso lowered the support of his left hand from the gun to pull out his handcuffs.

In a swift motion, Mandisa pushed the gun away with her left hand as her right hand pulled against the back side of the detective's wrist, forcing him to drop the gun. Mandisa struck Thabiso's throat with her open palm, then grabbed the back of his head and pulled it down to connect with her knee. Thabiso fell with a thud. "Later it is." She dug into the detective's pockets till she found his car keys. "Thank you detective." She rushed out of the house and into the vehicle parked outside. She lightly patted the back of her hood, the USB still in her hair. Satisfied, she turned the key in the ignition and drove off, a step closer to solving the biggest mystery of her life.

Glossary

AKASHONGO LUTHO – A Zulu phrase meaning "He/She didn't say anything"

Amufake estokisini – Zulu phrase meaning "put him in the back of a police vehicle"

And if awukwazi – A mix of English and Xhosa meaning "And if you can't". Switching between English and another language such as Xhosa or Zulu is quite common in South Africa.

Andifuni amanzi – A Xhosa phrase meaning "I don't want water"

Andiyazi – The Xhosa word for "I don't know"

APB – Short for all-points bulletin. This is typically a message to all police officers within a certain jurisdiction to be on the lookout for a suspect.

Bayaphila ekhaya? – A Zulu phrase meaning "Is everyone at home well?"

Bunga fanelanga uba pha – The Xhosa phrase meaning "You weren't supposed to be there"

Cha – The Zulu word meaning "No"

Dadewethu – Zulu word meaning "Sister"

Durbanite – a slang word for someone who was born or lives in Durban, a city in KwaZulu-Natal, South Africa.

Hamba – Zulu word meaning "Go"

Hayi – The Xhosa word for "No"

Hlisa umoya – The Xhosa phrase meaning "Calm down"

Kapteni – Zulu word for "Captain"

Kodwa sobabini siyayazi inintsi lento endiyicelayo – A Xhosa phrase meaning "But we both know that's a lot to ask for"

KUB City – KwaZulu Union Bay City

Lalela – The Zulu word for "Listen"

Lo mfana unesbindi – A Zulu phrase meaning "This boy is brave"

Luxoki obu – The Xhosa phrase meaning "That's a lie"

M.O. – The abbreviation of the Latin term "Modus Operandi" which refers to the habitual operations of an individual or group of people

Makazi – The Xhosa word for "Aunt"

Malumekazi – Zulu word for "Aunt"

Mamela – The Xhosa word for "Listen"

Mamela – The Xhosa word for "Listen"

Manje – The Zulu word for "Now"

Masambe – The Xhosa word for "Let's go"

Molo – The Xhosa word for "Hello"

Ndiyakuthanda – The Xhosa word for "I love you"

Ndiyeza – The Xhosa word for "I'm coming"

Neh? – A Xhosa expression meaning "right?"

Ngezibandayo – A Zulu slang word used in some parts of South Africa for alcohol.

Ngisakhona – A Zulu word for "I'm still here"

Ngiyabonga – Zulu word for "Thank you"

Ngiyaphila, unjani? – A Zulu phrase meaning "I'm well, how are you?"

Ngiyeza – A Zulu word meaning "I'm coming"

NgoMgqibelo – Zulu word for "Saturday"

Njengoba sibuya – A Zulu phrase meaning "On our way back".

Okwamanje – Zulu word meaning "For now"

Sisazo fika – The Xhosa phrase meaning "We're almost there"

Siyaphila sonke – A Zulu phrase meaning "We are all well"

So awuwazi – The Xhosa phrase meaning "So you don't know"

UB Incorporated – Union Bay Incorporated is a massive multi-industry conglomerate in Transportation, Agriculture, Property, Robotics and Environmental industries.

Ubaba – The Zulu word for "Dad"

Ubaba – Zulu word meaning "Father"

UBCB – Union Bay City Bank, a bank established before the founding of KwaZulu Union Bay City as a financial institution that the Founding Five could use. It quickly became the biggest and most trusted bank in Union Bay.

UBCN – Union Bay City News is the biggest news publishing house in KwaZulu Union Bay City.

UBNL – Union Bay Newsroom Live is a city owned broadcasting studio with its own television channel.

Umfazi – The Zulu word for "Woman"

Umsebenzi wam – A Xhosa phrase meaning "My job"

Uselele – Zulu word for he/she is asleep. It could also be used as a question.

USithole usebuyile? – A Zulu phrase meaning "Is Sithole back yet?"

Usuphelile u-petrol wakho – Zulu slag meaning "You have arrived"

Uswelekile – The Xhosa word for "He's dead"

Utheni? – The Xhosa word for "What's wrong?"

Utheni? – The Zulu word meaning "What did he/she say?"

Uthini – A Xhosa phrase meaning "What?"

Uyangithusa – The Zulu phrase for "You're scaring me"

Uyangithusa manje – The Zulu phrase for "You're scaring me now"

Uyanqena yini ukuvula iblog? – Zulu for "Are you too anxious to start a blog?"

Uzibulele – A Xhosa phrase meaning "He/she killed himself/herself"

Vula umnyango – A Xhosa phrase meaning "Open the door"

DUMO XABA NOVELS

COURT AFFAIRS
THE MAYOR IS DEAD!

Dingane Mkhize is a criminal defence lawyer who lives in the grey areas of the law and ethics.

After leaving the most prestigious law firm in KwaZulu Union Bay City, he built a reputation for himself by taking on difficult cases and never losing no matter what.

When he takes on a client being accused of the murder of the newly reinstated mayor, he starts to question the meaning of innocence.

Dingane must defend his client against one of the best lawyers of his former firm in a murder trial filled with complexities and surprises.

DUMO X POETRY ANTHOLOGIES

THE LEGACY

The Legacy is a self-reflective collection of poetry about Desolation, Fighting Doubt, Newfound Self-worth, Gratitude, Acceptance and Hope.

POETIC TYPE OF LOVE: Uthando Lwami

Poetic Type of Love: Uthando Lwami is a collection of poetry about, Finding Love, Fall Outs, Heartbreak, Accepting and Experiencing Love.